THE DAYSTAR VOYAGES

INVASION OF THE KILLER LOCUSTS

GILBERT MORRIS
AND DAN MEEKS

MOODY PRESS
CHICAGO

©1999 by
Gilbert Morris
and
Daniel Meeks

All rights reserved. No part of this book may be reproduced in any form without permission in writing from the publisher, except in the case of brief quotations embodied in critical articles or reviews.

All Scripture quotations, unless indicated, are taken from the *New American Standard Bible*, © 1960, 1962, 1963, 1968, 1971, 1972, 1973, 1975, 1977, and 1994 by The Lockman Foundation, La Habra, Calif. Used by permission.

ISBN: 0-8024-4110-6

1 3 5 7 9 10 8 6 4 2

Printed in the United States of America

This book is dedicated to my sister, Kelly Ann Sigman.

You put on immortality on Nov. 8, 1996. What a disastrous yet glorious event. I can't help but admire you. I love you very much. Meet me at the gate.

Characters

The *Daystar* ....an intergalactic star cruiser

The *Daystar* Space Rangers:

Jerusha Ericson, 15....a top-flight engineer
Raina St. Clair, 14.......the ship's communications officer
Mei-Lani Lao, 13 ....*Daystar*'s historian and linguist
Ringo Smith, 14...........a computer wizard
Heck Jordan, 15..........an electronics genius
Dai Bando, 16..............known for his exceptional physical abilities

The *Daystar* Officers:

Mark Edge ....*Daystar*'s young captain
Zeno Thrax..................the first officer
Bronwen Llewellen ....the navigator; Dai's aunt
Ivan Petroski...............the chief engineer
Temple Cole ....the flight surgeon
Tara Jaleel ....the weapons officer
Studs Cagney ....the crew chief

Contents

1

Contessa's Revenge

As the *Daystar* slipped through the darkness of space, flashing by giant glowing stars and black holes, Ranger Jerusha Ericson walked quickly down the corridor that ran the length of the cruiser.

She ran her hand along the shiny white surface of the inner wall and fancied she could feel the thrust of the powerful Mark V Star Drive engines that drove the spacecraft. This, she well knew, was probably all in her imagination. Even when under full power, these magnificent engines were quieter than those in any other intergalactic vessel that roamed the cosmos.

But Jerusha paused for a moment, leaned her weight against her hand, and fancied she could indeed feel a faint throbbing. Then her eyes moved to a space port. As always, she took pleasure in the display of glittering stars that decorated the blackness of space. A smile turned up the corners of her lips, as it came to her that she had never seen a picture, or heard a symphony, or read a book that compared with the art that she was now looking at—the handiwork of God as He had made it.

Just then Studs Cagney, carrying the barrel of a proton cannon, started to brush by her. But then he stopped and grinned. "You ain't gonna get your job done that way, Jerusha."

Studs was a short, muscular man with thinning black hair and intensely dark eyes. With his free hand he reached over and tugged at her hair, saying, "Like I always said, a woman ought to be home washing dishes and cooking for her man."

Jerusha laughed for she was accustomed to Studs's rough kidding. She knew that he was really very fond of her, as she was of him. As she started to walk on, she returned his grin, saying, "A woman has to catch a man first before she can cook for him."

"Aw, you won't have no trouble," Studs assured her. Then he lifted his hand in a quick farewell gesture and marched down the long corridor in the other direction.

Indeed Jerusha Ericson should have no trouble "catching a man," for the fifteen year old was already very attractive. Her ash blonde hair hung down to her shoulders, and her blue eyes were so dark that sometimes they even looked black. They were set in a squarish face, and at five ten she was strong and athletic.

As flight engineer of the space cruiser *Daystar*, Jerusha Ericson was as intelligent as she was attractive. In fact, usually the only fault that people found in Jerusha was that perhaps she was too competitive. She simply hated to lose at anything, and sometimes she could not conceal the anger that flashed out when she lost.

She had just started to walk on, when she encountered another crew member, Ivan Petroski, the chief engineer and her immediate boss. Petroski was a dwarf, no more than four feet six, but he was extremely well proportioned. He had brown eyes and thick brown hair. All the people on his planet, Belinka Two, were about his small size, he said. Indeed, he often boasted that he was one of the tallest of the men there.

"Jerusha, go relieve Heck in Engineering," he told her. "He should have been finished with the relay diagnostics thirty minutes ago. Captain Edge needs the final checks performed before we power up the Neutro cannon." Ivan scratched his forearm. "I don't know why we need the thing anyway. It's old technology. But anyway, get yourself down there and light a fire under him!"

"Right, Chief. I'll get right to it," Jerusha replied cheerfully.

She walked even more quickly now and within minutes had arrived at the Engineering section, where she spoke the password.

Engineering's door was connected to a voice lock, and, recognizing Jerusha's voice, it opened for her. She'd often thought that this was like no door that most people had ever seen, for it expanded like the pupil of one's eye. From a small, almost invisible dot, the opening widened and widened until she was able to step through—just in time to hear a wild scream:

"Help! Help! Somebody get this monster off of me!"

Jerusha's eyes flew to a scene that caused her to both frown and sigh. There on the floor, Heck Jordan was lying flat on his back, holding one hand over his face and still crying out for help in a muffled scream. Poised above him was Jerusha Ericson's enormous black German shepherd.

Contessa had been with Jerusha since she was nothing but a pup. The dog was actually a super German shepherd. She had been bred for intelligence and strength. She could smell things that no other dog could smell, and her powerful, muscular jaws could crunch anything that was not actually tool steel. Her enormous teeth were enough to take off Heck's arm, but the dog was actually very gentle.

At the moment, Contessa was keeping her front paws planted on the Space Ranger's chest while she nipped at something that he waved frantically in his right hand.

"Heck, have you been teasing Contessa again?"

Wildly, Heck turned his eyes toward Jerusha and began to plead, "Get her off of me, will you, please?"

"You *have* been teasing her, haven't you?"

The dog seemed to be enjoying the whole thing. She continued to nibble at the candy bar in Heck's hand. She paused from time to time to lick his face.

Jerusha gazed down at the two of them and said, "You sure know how to pick the wrong type of man, Contessa. Now, what's all this about, Heck?"

Heck Jordan kept on squirming and wiggling. But the weight of the dog held him down. And if he twisted too much, she simply reached out and seized his arm between her powerful jaws and held him down.

Finally Heck whined, "This vicious animal is trying to get revenge." He tugged at his arm, but it was as firmly fixed between Contessa's jaws as if in a vise. "Tell her to turn me loose, will you? Please, Jerusha? Pretty please?"

"First, you tell me what happened."

"Well, I was just teasing her a little bit with this candy bar. I'd pretend to give her a bite, then I would eat it myself. And then—for no reason at all—she just jumped on me and knocked me down and started eating my candy bar. She's been licking my face at the same time! Now look at me! I got these slimy candy remains all over me! Get me out of this, Jerusha!"

Jerusha tried to frown, but the sight of Heck lying under Contessa and with candy smeared all over his face was simply too much for her. She laughed aloud. Then she spoke to the dog. "Well, come on, Contessa, let the big baby up. But you'll have to apologize to her first, Heck."

Heck squirmed at this, but he finally mumbled, "I'm sorry, Contessa."

"And tell her you won't do it again."

"I won't ever do it again. Now get her off me!"

Contessa backed off at once at Jerusha's command.

Heck said, "Give me a hand up, will you?"

Jerusha, still laughing, reached for his arms to help him up.

But as she did, Heck let out a shrill snicker. She was taken totally off guard, and before she could stop him, he had rubbed his chocolate-smeared cheeks all over hers.

"Get away from me!" Jerusha yelled.

She pushed at Heck. He took a step backwards. The German shepherd bared her fangs, and a warning growl sounded deep in her throat.

"Keep that monster off of me!" Heck squawked. But he was laughing at the same time.

Heck was a heavyset boy with bright red hair and innocent-looking blue eyes. He was an electronics genius, but he had several serious problems. He was constantly eating something, usually sweets. And Heck Jordan was without doubt the most selfish young man that any of the other Space Rangers had ever met. He alone among the group was not a Christian, and he resisted anyone's speaking to him on the subject.

He loved fancy clothes, too, and—since he was color-blind—he made a truly spectacular appearance most of the time. Knotted around his throat today was a lime green neckerchief that ill suited his uniform. Standing and laughing at Jerusha, who like himself was now streaked with chocolate, he made a ludicrous picture. Fortunately for Heck, dress rules on the *Daystar* were relaxed.

"That's what you get for laughing at me, Jerusha!"

Jerusha scrubbed at her cheeks furiously and then looked down at the chocolate on her hands. "I ought to let Contessa bite your fingers right off!" she snapped.

"Aw, don't be mad, Jerusha. Tell you what, I'll meet you after duty and give you a break. I know you got a real yen for me, so—"

Jerusha shoved him toward the door, saying, "Heck, just go clean up. Ivan says I'm to replace you until you report to the captain. And try to find something besides that hideous rag that you've got around your neck! It makes me ill!"

2
A Word of Wisdom

Dai Bando and his aunt, Navigator Bronwen Llewellen, were about as different in appearance as two human beings could get.

Bronwen Llewellen was fifty-two years old and had beautiful silver hair and large, dark blue eyes. She was small and well preserved for her years, and traces of a youthful beauty still clung to her.

Dai Bando was sixteen. The boy was almost six feet tall. He had a perfect build that enabled him to easily perform almost anything requiring physical skills. He had the strength, agility, and quickness of an acrobat—which indeed he had once been. His black hair and black eyes were as dark as anything in nature. Two prominent dimples appeared on his cheeks when he smiled, which was often.

Aunt Bronwen sat knitting. They were in her cabin and had been talking about the *Daystar*'s last mission—to the planet Morlandria, where they had done battle with Zaria, the Queen of Darkness. But Dai was having trouble keeping his mind on what was being said.

Her eyes grew troubled as she talked on. "If ever I saw evil concentrated in one human being, it was in that woman. And I've seen some wicked men and women during my many years, Dai. But nothing like her. It's as if something had been left out of her—the goodness that you usually find in even the worst of people. Zaria was pure evil as far as I could see."

His aunt sighed, then continued her knitting. It

was an ancient skill that she apparently loved to perform. She had made scarves and even sweaters for all the Space Rangers. Her fingers perhaps were a bit stiffer than they used to be, but still the needles clicked busily as she talked on about their adventure with the dark queen.

Dai was a quiet young man, perhaps the quietest of any of the Space Rangers. He had once told his aunt, "I'm not supersmart like the other Rangers, Aunt. I'm just average. All of them are so smart they just scare me sometimes." However, it was to Dai they all looked when any physical crisis arose, and he knew that.

And today the mind of Bronwen Llewellen's favorite nephew was far away.

He saw her glancing at him from time to time with something like worry in her eyes. She seemed to know that something was distracting his thoughts, even though he was trying to be polite, as always.

After a while Bronwen asked, "What are you thinking about, Dai?"

Caught off guard by the sudden question, Dai Bando blinked, and he knew his answer was somewhat lame. "Why, I suppose I was thinking about how you were able to deal with Zaria—wisely, confidently, without fear. I always felt that somehow there was something very . . . very strong . . . in her."

"Yes, there was. Evil can be very powerful."

"But you were able to stand against her, Aunt." Dai leaned forward, and he frowned as he continued to think about the spiritual struggles that had taken place on their mission to Morlandria. Finally he shook his head. "That's not me. I'd never be able to do anything like that."

Dropping the knitting needles in her lap, the woman gripped his shoulder and said quietly, "Dai, I want to warn you about something."

"Warn me?" He gave her a puzzled look. "About what?"

"I want to warn you about trying to make yourself into someone else."

"I'm not sure I understand what you mean."

"I've seen you do this before. You talk about Ringo and how he can run a computer. Or you talk about how good Heck is with electronics. And you talk about Raina—that she's so wonderful with communications."

"You might as well add Mei-Lani," Dai said. "She knows just about everything you can find in books, and she's only thirteen!"

"There, you see? You're doing it again! It's the sort of thing Ringo does all the time, too! I don't think you are being fair to yourself."

"But I really do feel so left behind. You don't know what it's like, Aunt, to be the dumbest one in the class."

"In the first place, you are not *dumb!* Stop saying that!"

"But the rest of the Rangers—"

"Never mind the rest of the Rangers! You're not the rest of the Rangers. You're Dai Bando, and you're exactly what God made you to be. Do you think God makes mistakes?"

"No, of course not."

"Then stop blaming God because you're not like Ringo, or Raina, or Jerusha. You're Dai Bando, and God has made you the way you are for a very specific purpose. I don't think you understand, Dai, how many people in the world would do almost anything to be as strong and quick as you are."

Dai did not answer for a moment, but he disagreed with his aunt. He saw his physical strength and quickness and courage as nothing nearly as special as the abilities the other Rangers had. Finally he muttered, "I'm not as quick as Contessa."

Bronwen Llewellen laughed out loud. First she shook him, and then she shook her head from side to side. "So now you're comparing yourself with a dog! Forevermore, Dai, don't you see what you're doing? You're saying, 'God, You didn't make me right. I've only got two legs, and Contessa has four. Therefore, she's better than I am.'"

Dai suddenly laughed, too. He couldn't help it. "That's not exactly right, Aunt. I really wouldn't want to be a dog."

"Then don't put yourself down because you can't do math as well as Jerusha, for example. That's what God put into her. We need flight engineers. But we need what you have, too, Dai. There wouldn't be any Ringo Smith if you hadn't been there to save him. You remember when he was attacked by that horrible monster on our first mission?"

"Well, anybody would have done that."

"Most people could *not* have done that! It was because God gave you special strength and skill that you were able to save his life."

Dai did not much like to be complimented, and he suspected that his face was turning a dusky red. "Well . . . still . . . that wasn't too much." But he did know that his aunt was genuinely concerned about her young nephew. Dai's father, her brother, had been very close to her before his death, and she had promised God always to do all she could to help Dai along his way.

"Dai, you've got to learn that the Lord is going to work out His purpose in your life. He's going to take care of all the details, so I want you to stop worrying about what you are able to do and what you can't do."

"I'll try, Aunt Bronwen."

"Another thing," she said, picking up the knitting needles again, "it wouldn't hurt you to spend a little fun time with the other Space Rangers. You work hard all the time, and you spend more time with Studs Cagney than you do with your younger friends."

"But what's wrong with that?"

"I think you do it because Studs is more your kind of person. Somewhat of a loner. But he's also no threat to you, for you sense you're more intelligent than he is."

"Studs is a nice guy! I like him a lot."

"Of course, he is. I like him myself. What I'm saying is, it's not healthy for you to avoid the people you think are better than you in some way. When you look in your mirror, say, 'God, You made me just like this. I don't need blond hair or red hair, because You gave me black hair for a reason. And I don't need to be anything I'm not, either, because You've made me just the way I am for a special purpose.'"

"Strong back and a weak mind," Dai said, but he put up his hands in defense when he saw the look in his aunt's eyes. "Just kidding, Aunt. I'll try to do what you say." He hesitated, then said, "But I sure wish God would tell me what He's up to in my life."

"We all wish that." She nodded. "Just remember the Bible verse that we memorized together—'God causes all things to work together for good to those who love God, to those who are called according to His purpose.' Say that over and over to yourself, and when you're feeling down say, 'This isn't my plan—it's God's plan.'"

"All right, Aunt Bronwen, I'll do it. Now I guess I'll go have some of that fun you want me to have."

"Good!" She gave him a quick, flashing smile. "Your enthusiasm wouldn't have anything to do with one of those attractive young ladies, would it? I never can figure out whether you like Raina or Jerusha the best."

He grinned back at her. “I can’t figure it out, either. They’re both nice girls, aren’t they?”

“They are, indeed, and they’ll appreciate a word from a handsome young man like you. Get off with you now. Go and have your fun.”

Mei-Lani Lao was the youngest of the Space Rangers. She was Oriental, and her hair was as black as that of Dai Bando, and her eyes were warm and brown. She was a very small girl, barely over five feet and weighing only ninety-five pounds, but what she lacked in size she made up for in brains. She had the reputation of being practically a genius at history. She could quote the ancient poets and philosophers. But Mei-Lani’s extra-special gift was in languages. It was a constant source of astonishment to her friends that she could learn a language almost as easily as they could learn a new song.

Raina St. Clair sat beside Mei-Lani at the Communications console, working on the project that Zeno Thrax, the first officer, had given them.

The Communications console was composed of a vast array of multicolored lights and switches. To the untrained eye, its design seemed totally incomprehensible, but both Raina and Mei-Lani had spent many training hours at the Space Academy using this very style of device.

The girls’ fingers manipulated the switches effortlessly. It was a good thing, too. Thrax wanted them to break the Lo’custra language. So far, they weren’t having much luck. Unfortunately, Mei-Lani said it was a language unlike anything she had ever heard before.

But Raina St. Clair could not keep her mind on the problem. She was a year older than Mei-Lani but with auburn hair and a widow’s peak and light green eyes.

Her oval face was very fair, and she had a cleft in her chin, which she desperately hated. She had even considered surgery to correct what she saw as a problem. But then Bronwen Llewellen had given her the same sermon that she gave everyone else: "God had a purpose in making you as you are."

Physically, Raina was rather frail. As a matter of fact, she had never completely recovered emotionally from the loss of her parents when their house burned down. Her father had died in saving her. She usually tried to put those sad memories out of her mind, but even now—as her hands flew over the console—she seemed to see her father's face as he grabbed her, his skin already singed by the flames. She shut her eyes to close out that vision and desperately tried to change her train of thought.

As thoughts of her parents faded, though, another face began to swim vaguely around. Then it came sharply into focus. The face was that of Dai Bando. His black, curly hair was falling over his forehead. His dark eyes were smiling at her.

It was not the first time that Raina St. Clair had thought of Dai Bando. She was becoming quite conscious of boys. On the one hand, she knew this was normal, and yet somehow it troubled her. But she often said to herself, *If I have to think about a boy, there couldn't be a nicer one than Dai Bando to think about.*

Aside from Bronwen Llewellen, Raina was probably the most devout Christian on the whole cruiser. She read the Bible so often that its most familiar verses had become inscribed on her mind. And of all the Rangers, she probably was the most careful about not letting herself do anything wrong. She knew that at times she seemed almost self-righteous, but she wanted so desperately to please her Savior—and her parents, who had had great hopes for her—that she was determined to walk with God.

Now, however, as Raina worked on the language problem, her mind continued to go back to Dai. Suddenly she asked, as casually as she could, "Mei-Lani, what do you think of Dai?"

The smaller girl turned to her, probably knowing what was in the mind of her friend. She was very sharp, this Mei-Lani. And though Raina had tried to hide her interest in the tall, dark young man, Mei-Lani must have sensed that her apparent disinterest was all an act.

"I think, Raina, that Dai is very different from most boys his age."

"Well, he's better looking than most, and stronger, and quicker, and I never saw anyone with as much courage."

"Yes, he's all that," Mei-Lani admitted. "What I meant, though, was that he's not really interested in girls. You take Ringo and Heck—they are, even though Ringo tries to cover it up." Then she said, "As a matter of fact, Ringo's got quite a crush on you."

"Oh, *that* doesn't amount to anything." Raina waved her hand in a nervous gesture.

"I think it does to Ringo. He's very shy, and he's had a rough life, you know. I wish you'd pay more attention to him."

"Why, we do a lot of things together! But I was asking about Dai. What do you mean he's not like other boys?"

"I just think he's not ready for romance right now. You know, it's like with reading. You can't teach anyone to read until they're ready. My sister didn't read until she was nearly seven, but I was reading when I was four. Today, she can read as well as I can. We just started at different times."

Raina gave her an odd look. It was one of the rare occasions on which Mei-Lani even mentioned her family. She was usually strangely silent about them. But Raina was interested more in what Mei-Lani was saying about Dai. "Why should he not be interested in romance? He's old enough. He's sixteen."

"Well, sometimes boys are sort of slow in that way, I think. Sometimes when they're sixteen years old chronologically, they're only about twelve years old in the way they think."

Raina laughed suddenly. "You don't have a very high opinion of boys, do you?"

"They're just what they are. That's what I'm trying to tell you. Right now Dai is interested in other things. He likes to be with the men of the crew. He likes to do things with Zeno Thrax and with Studs Cagney. He's also interested in the Bible and spiritual things—which is unusual for a boy his age. He's just not really much interested in girls, Raina. He's interested in other things. "

Raina turned back to the console, and the two continued to work on the language puzzle. She did not say anything for a long time. She was thinking, *Mei-Lani just doesn't understand. She acts even younger than thirteen. Sometimes she acts about nine. She's always been so smart that people treat her as an adult, but she's not. She's still just a little girl inside.*

The two were still busy at work when suddenly a voice said, "Hi, girls!" Raina and Mei-Lani both looked around as Dai Bando walked in.

As always, he looked neat as a pin, Raina thought. He wore the standard Space Ranger uniform—slate gray tunic with silver trim on the collar and above the cuffs. The ensign insignia was located on the right sleeve and the *Daystar* Space Ranger insignia on the left. He wore navy pants that had a silver stripe down the side. Completing the uniform, he had on a pair of black half boots with rubber soles.

Raina always thought he looked so handsome in his uniform. She almost swooned as she looked at him.

And then he came over to stand directly between them and said, “Raina, why don’t you come over to the crew lounge later? Maybe we can play chess or something until supper—then eat together.”

Raina knew the stunned look on her face had to be almost comical. It was the first time that Dai had ever asked her to do anything—just the two of them. Quickly she tried to wipe the astonished expression from her face and smiled. “Why, that sounds like fun, Dai. I’ll see you there in about an hour.”

“Good. Take it easy, girls. Bye-bye.” He turned and walked away, humming under his breath.

Raina looked at Mei-Lani and grinned. “Now, there goes your theory.”

“Maybe so.” Mei-Lani shrugged. “But I’ll believe it when I see it.” She frowned slightly, then said, “Don’t make too much out of one date, Raina.”

“Oh, I won’t,” Raina said, but inside her heart was singing. *He’s interested in me! He really likes me, or he wouldn’t have asked me for a date.* She was so pleased and so excited that she could not keep her mind on the language problem at all. At last she said, “I think I’ll go get ready.”

She got up to leave.

“You’ve got fifty minutes!” Mei-Lani protested. “You can’t take that long to make yourself prettier!”

But Raina was gone.

3

Ordered into Harm's Way

Somehow it had always seemed to Capt. Mark Edge that the commander of the Intergalactic Council should be a man—and a strong man at that.

He sat looking at his superior officer, Commandant Winona Lee, and he thought, *I sure would never pick her out in a crowd as being the head of the entire battle fleet of the Intergalactic force.*

Indeed, Commandant Lee was not impressive insofar as size and physical strength were concerned. She was a small-framed woman of exactly fifty years. She had silver gray hair. She was trimly built and still retained traces of earlier good looks. But it was in her steady gray eyes that the force of her mind and will were revealed.

Captain Edge and the Commandant sat on the bridge of the *Daystar*. The captain had just greeted his superior officer and had received her compliments on the cruiser's last mission.

"The Council was very pleased with your mission to Morlandria, Captain Edge."

"Thank you, Commandant. Unfortunately, the assignment turned out to be a little more difficult than I had anticipated."

"Missions have a way of doing that." A smile turned up the corners of the commandant's lips. Then she leaned forward to say quietly, "And were you entirely satisfied with the performance of the crew?"

"Why, of course, Commandant."

"And the *Daystar* Space Rangers?" Again a smile touched her lips. "You were hesitant to take such young people onto your crew, as I recall. Did they come up to your expectations?"

Mark Edge felt his face color. He well remembered how he—and most of the crew—had spoken rather lightly of the Space Rangers at the beginning. But then he grinned. "I'll have to admit that they performed very well, indeed!"

"I'm glad to hear it, Captain." There was a pause, and then Commandant Lee asked innocently, as if the matter were of no great importance, "And your surgeon —Dr. Cole—were you satisfied with her performance also?"

Quickly Edge looked up, searching the commandant's face. He did not know how, but the woman seemed to be aware of everything that went on aboard the *Daystar*. It appeared even now, as he studied her features, that there was knowledge in her eyes that he could not account for. And he really didn't want his commanding officer to know that he was romantically involved with one of his crew.

Stiffly he said, "Why, of course, Commandant. Dr. Cole has more than exceeded the requirements of her duties."

"It's always good to hear that sort of thing." Again there was the slight pause, then again she said innocently, "She is very attractive as well. I suppose that doesn't hurt on long voyages."

"I hadn't really noticed."

"I'm surprised that you haven't. She is an attractive young lady indeed, and your reputation has preceded you in matters of the heart."

Edge was dimly aware that, all around them, the normal activities of the ship were going on. But all he could think of at the moment was that, somehow or other, Commandant Lee was looking directly into his mind.

It's like I have plate glass on my forehead, he thought. *Sometimes it seems she even knows what I'm thinking.* Finally, in desperation, he changed the subject. "I'm hoping the *Daystar* crew can get a little R and R now, Commandant."

Immediately, a slight furrow disturbed Commandant Lee's brow. She sighed and said, "I would like nothing better than to order rest and relaxation for your crew as a reward for the fine job you did on Morlandria. But regrettably, Mark, that will not be possible."

"Another mission?"

She looked through the port and far into the distance. "I'm afraid so, Captain." Then the commandant turned back to fully face him, and a more official tone came into her voice. "Have you ever heard of the plant Capella?"

"No, I don't believe I have."

"It orbits the star Algol."

Edge searched his memory. "Algol. If I remember right, doesn't that mean 'head of the demon'? I believe one of my Academy instructors called it the 'Demon Star.' Don't tell me you're sending us to the demon home world!"

"Algol is nothing like that." Commandant Lee smiled, perhaps making a mental note to herself to pay closer attention to the Space Academy curriculum. "Capella is a beautiful planet inhabited by tribal nations. For the most part, its citizens have lived in peace for thousands of years."

Edge listened carefully as Commandant Lee described what he knew would be their next destination. Then he asked, "What's the big problem there? I'm sure there's something."

"Communications have stopped coming from Capella, but their last transmission pleaded for military help from the Galactic Command. I want you to investigate at once."

"What do you expect me to find there?"

"Trouble. Nothing but trouble." The age lines on Commandant Lee's face were even more pronounced now. She sighed again, leaned back in her chair, and asked, "Are you a good student of history, Captain?"

"Well, I didn't set the curve, if that's what you mean. But why, Commandant? Do I need to know some history to go to Capella?"

"Yes, you do. Before you arrive, you need to have a firm grasp on what's been happening in that sector. Now, listen carefully, Mark. In the first place, there has been a civil war brewing on Capella for the last few years."

"Same old story? The have-nots wanting to take away from the haves? That's usually the story of a civil war."

"But not this time." The commandant did smile then—for just a moment. She said, "It's about a woman."

"A civil war over a woman? It sounds like something out of the old myths—the Trojan War fought over Helen."

"Not quite like that, Captain. It's like this: The suzerain, as they call their chief leader, is a man named Brutarius. His family has ruled Capella for thousands of years, and up until recently the other tribes seemed to be content with his reign. But his wife—her name is Anmoir—never gave him a son. Sixteen years ago, however, she gave birth to a female."

Edge nodded instantly. "Ah, I think I see the problem. I gather that the other tribes do not take kindly to being ruled by a woman suzerain."

"And you are exactly right. Primarily the Fenian tribe objects. Lord Miterlan, who is over the Fenians, led the revolt. They say they simply will not have a woman as the next suzerain, and civil war has already broken out over the matter."

"So Brutarius has got to defend his suzerainty—and his family's rule. I suppose our first job is to stop the civil war?"

"No, that won't be necessary. That war stopped when the Lo'custra invaded."

Captain Edge felt his mind growing slightly dizzy. "The Lo'custra. Who are *they?*"

"No one seems to know much about them—and for a very good reason. Whatever they are—they appear to be nonhuman—they leave no witnesses. They strike, kill everything that has breath, and very few have ever lived to tell about it. They appear to have no respect for any creature except their own kind."

"Where do they—exactly what are your orders, Commandant?"

"I will have to leave you with a very flexible set of orders, Captain, because I have no idea what you will find. While you are investigating, I will prepare the fleet to rescue Capella from these Lo'custra creatures, but in the meantime you will just have to hold the line."

"We are to engage the enemy?"

"Only if necessary. It is important that Capella be saved, and if you must fight to do that, then so be it. It's a dangerous mission. And I want your scouting reports as soon as possible."

"Understood, Commandant. Any other orders?"

"I have discussed this mission with Captain

Pursey, my starship captain," she said. "He was very impressed with the way the *Daystar* Space Rangers handled the mission on Morlandria. Both of us have every confidence of the Rangers' ability—and in yours, of course, Captain—to deal with the Capella situation."

"We'll do the best we can. When would you like for us to leave?"

"At once. There's no time to be lost. People may be dying right now from the attacks of the Lo'custra. Whoever they are."

Raina stood in the middle of her cabin and stared at the clothes that were strewn about. Despair was in her eyes, and her lips were drawn up in an expression of displeasure. She gathered up a lime green dress, held it up against herself, and went over to the mirror. She studied the dress critically for a moment, then threw it on the floor.

"It's hideous! I couldn't wear that thing to a dogfight!" She had never seen a dogfight, but she had heard Studs Cagney occasionally use the expression, and it seemed fitting.

One by one she gathered up the garments. In truth, there were not very many—only three to be exact. Most of the time, the crew wore their uniforms, which were attractive enough. They were allowed to carry only three changes of civilian dress.

For the third time she picked up a powder blue outfit, slipped into it, and stood twisting around trying to see how she looked from the back. This was difficult, for she had only a mirror that was no more than one-foot wide by two-feet high. She could never see all of herself at once in it. This had not been a problem for Raina in the past, for she was not vain at all—at least, she never had been considered so before now.

Somehow the invitation from Dai to go with him on what amounted to a date had changed her. Usually Raina prayed over most decisions, no matter how small. Her parents had helped her develop that habit when she was very young. But this time the prayer habit had been pushed aside—not deliberately, of course. She was just more excited than she could ever remember being in her entire life.

As she twisted and turned, trying to see herself in the small mirror, the image of Dai Bando still floated into her mind—his black hair, and black eyes, and white teeth against his tanned skin.

"He is the handsomest thing I've ever seen," she said aloud, "and he's good too! You don't find that combination in a boy very often." *Often*, she thought, *when people are very attractive, it seems they get conceited and egotistical. But Dai's not like that.*

Finally in a fit of despair, she yanked off the blue dress and put on the last one. She had also tried on this one several times. She had thought it was an attractive outfit when she saw it in the shop. It consisted of a short gold skirt and a dark maroon top. It fitted her well enough, but she stood staring into the mirror, dissatisfied with it, anyway.

She scowled and pulled it off again, and then she was interrupted by a knock at the door.

"Wait a minute," she said. She grabbed for a robe and put it on quickly. "All right, come in!"

Jerusha Ericson entered. She was wearing her uniform, and she looked very strong and athletic, as usual. Her blue eyes were alight with interest as she said, "What's this I hear about you and Dai going out on a date?"

Staring at her friend, Raina demanded suspiciously, "How did *you* find out about it, Jerusha?"

"Why, I heard Dai turning down a sparring match with Lieutenant Jaleel."

Tara Jaleel, weapons officer aboard the *Daystar*, was an expert in the martial arts and had thoroughly thrashed everyone on board—except Dai Bando. He was so fast and strong that she was never able to defeat him. Raina knew that Dai did not particularly enjoy the martial arts, but he considered it part of his duty, and usually he willingly sparred with Jaleel when she asked.

"What did he say? Tell me!" Raina begged. "What did he say?"

"Why, he just said that he had asked you to meet him at the lounge after duty today. Now, what *is* all this? I didn't know you and Dai were interested in each other."

Raina suddenly found herself unable to speak. Her attachment to Dai had been mostly a secret. She was well aware that anything like this would let a girl in for a tremendous amount of teasing on board ship. And besides, up until now she had had no idea that Dai was interested in her.

"Oh, it's just nothing much," she managed. "He came into the Communications room and just asked me to meet him in the crew lounge to play chess or something."

Jerusha looked around at the clothes strewn on the floor, and then her eyes came back to Raina. "It looks like you're making plenty of preparation."

"I don't have a thing to wear but these old rags!"

"Old rags? Why, you bought all of these just before we left on our last mission. They're *all* nice."

"Really? Do you really think so, Jerusha?"

"Why, of course, I do. Here, I'll tell you what. You

try each one of them on, and I'll tell you which one I like the best. Then I'll help you with your hair."

The two girls immediately began the process of selecting the dress that was the least hideous in Raina's sight. Finally, by some magic, Jerusha Ericson convinced her that the powder blue was made for her and made her look very beautiful indeed.

As she was working on Raina's hair, Jerusha said casually, "Can I say something to you, Raina?"

"Of course."

"I'm a year older than you. I know that's not very much, but I've found out one thing that you may not have bumped into yet—something about boys, I mean."

"Yes, what is it?"

"Don't take a date too seriously. Girls are always prone to take things more seriously than boys, anyway." She paused while she carefully placed a strand of Raina's auburn hair exactly as she wanted it. Then she said, "I remember I got my hopes built up over a boy once. I thought he was interested in me, but he really wasn't. I got very upset with him, but really it was not his fault at all. It was mine."

"Oh, I'll be careful."

"Good, then. I just wanted to be sure you didn't take all this too seriously."

Raina said only, "I'll be very careful."

But at the same time she was saying this, her hopes were rising steadily. *He likes me!* she thought with delight. *He likes me! I know he does! Dai Bando likes me very much, or he wouldn't have asked to play chess with me!*

4
A Golden Glow

Dai Bando purposefully made his way along the corridor that led to the computer library. As he stepped inside, he was pleased to see that Ringo Smith was there, sitting at the controls.

"Hi, Ringo."

Ringo looked up and grinned. "Hello, Dai. I don't see you here very often."

Ringo Smith had brown hair and hazel eyes. Everyone was aware that the boy had had a rough life, having been raised in a state orphanage. Even now as he smiled at Dai, he absently fingered a medallion suspended around his neck by a leather thong. Dai knew it bore the image of a hawk or falcon on one side. He knew that on the other side was the profile of a strong-looking man and some sort of motto written in an exotic language.

Dai also knew that Ringo had not learned to trust people. The boy didn't really know how to give or receive love. Still, he was one of the most pleasant of the *Daystar* crew.

"What can I do for you today, Dai?" Ringo asked.

"I need a little help, Ringo. I'm not very good with computers and things like that, and I would like to know something about this place where we're going on our next mission."

"Oh, sure. The Perseus sector."

Ringo sent the appropriate inquiries to the library computer.

"There's just the normal constellation stuff mostly," he announced a moment later. Then he continued reading the data. "There's information here about the star Algol—its magnitude and distance data. There are quite a few blinking stars in this sector."

"What do you mean, 'blinking' stars?"

"They really don't blink at all. They just appear to if you're looking at them through a telescope on Earth," Ringo commented as he continued examining the list. "Oh, here we go. The planet Capella. It's the only inhabitable planet orbiting Algol."

Dai leaned closer. "Let's look at that."

The boys studied the screen diligently for a time, and then the beeper on Ringo's belt sounded.

"Smith—report to me at once!"

"There's my lord and master," Ringo said. "I've got to get down to Engineering."

Ivan Petroski was a fiery, short-tempered man, as they both knew, and Ringo scurried out of the computer room. He called back over his shoulder, "If you need more help with the computer, just give me a call! I'll get back as soon as I can!"

"Right! Thanks a lot, Ringo."

Sitting before the massive array of dials and controls, Dai Bando felt totally helpless. He was practically computer illiterate and desperately wished that, instead of being a singer and an athlete of great talent, he had some ability with such technology as this. He was actually afraid to touch any of the controls, although Ringo had told him, "You can't do any harm except to turn it off. Just try to remember the few rules that I gave you."

Cautiously Dai touched the knob that scrolled the information over the large screen glowing in front of him. He breathed a sigh of relief when nothing bad happened, and then he began to read the data that was displayed.

For a time it was fairly boring, simply giving a history of the planet Capella and the royal family. But at last he got to the more recent history and sat up a little straighter as the image of a very young child began to appear.

"So that's Sanara," Dai murmured, and he smiled at the first pictures. He had learned that she was the daughter of the suzerain and his wife. The first images were little more than baby pictures such as any parents would take of their child when she was still an infant. He scrolled through these rapidly, thinking, *Mothers and fathers are all the same everywhere. They take millions of pictures of the first child and then not many of the second.*

But scrolling through the pictures was pleasant enough. In fact, it was a little like magic to watch the infant rapidly grow into a little girl. He smiled as she went through the process of losing her teeth. In one picture she grinned at the camera, not at all conscious of the big gap in her smile as she would have been had she been older.

She learned to ride a tricycle, then a bicycle, and with each image she grew a little bigger. She was an attractive child and vivacious. He was listening to the accompanying audio and noted that the girl always seemed to be singing—songs that Dai had never before heard, however. This did interest him, for, even as a child, she had a clear voice. He wondered if as a young woman she was still able to sing.

The pictured child grew taller then and passed out of childhood. And at that point Dai reached a place in the film that startled him.

Sanara had been strolling about the palace, as he

supposed, when she walked right up to the visual recorder and smiled. For some reason, her smile had quite an unexpected effect on Dai.

"She sure is a pretty thing," he murmured. He knew from the information that she was sixteen years old. In the picture her bright, golden hair cascaded down in layers to her neck and then to her shoulders. Her skin, he could tell, was very smooth and was a rich, golden tan. She had large, expressive brown eyes and a generous mouth. In fact, she was one of the most attractive girls that Dai had ever seen.

But it was not only her beauty that drew him, although he certainly noticed that.

He somehow sensed from her expression that the suzerain's daughter had a genuine love for people and was devoted to helping them. How Dai knew this he could never explain. He suddenly thought of his Aunt Llewellen. She could take one look at a person, it seemed to Dai, and know exactly what was inside of him. She had once told him, "The Welsh are like that sometimes. I think you have a little of it yourself."

And now as he looked at the face of the girl who smiled back at him from the screen, he *knew* that she was, indeed, very gentle, despite being the daughter of the ruler of the planet. He knew also that she was very unassuming.

He leaned back and studied her beautiful face for a while. It was pleasant to sit there, alone, relaxed, and watching the screen before him.

Dai had not thought he was tired. His endurance was always incredible. He had slept well the previous night, too, so there was no reason for his dozing off. But for some reason his eyelids began to grow heavy. And at some point, reality changed into a dream.

Dai found himself walking into the scene that had

been playing on the screen before him. But he was intensely aware that what he was now seeing was nothing that had been recorded in the computer library. Indeed, the computer screen was still flickering, but he knew he was dreaming.

He saw Sanara. She was climbing very quickly up a steep mountain. She was wearing a silver garment consisting of a tunic and trousers that seemed to be caught up around the ankles with elastic. Over her breast was a symbol that marked the royal family, and her golden hair fell loosely about her shoulders as she struggled upward.

Dai sensed that the girl was using all of her strength, and, seeing her face very clearly, he knew that she was desperately afraid. He looked around, seeking the source of her fear.

And there in the dusky distance, clouded with fog, he could see sinister figures rapidly approaching. They were so clothed in the darkness of the fog that he could not quite make them out, but he knew instinctively that they were ugly and frightful.

When Sanara reached the mountaintop, she stood looking around as if expecting help to come, but there was nothing. Dai seemed aware of the height of the peak. He was also aware that no one was coming to her rescue.

In his dream, he now was standing only a few feet away from her. The girl looked very small—Dai was almost six feet, and she was no more than five feet tall. Her lips moved. He thought that she must be praying, although he could not hear what was being said. There was no smile on Sanara's face now.

Dai looked downward. He saw that alien figures were starting to climb the peak toward them from every direction. He had no doubt that they meant harm to the girl. And there was nowhere for her to go. As he watched, she fled behind a small hut, but that offered not much protection at all. He followed her.

And then Sanara dropped to her knees and started praying aloud. Dai could hear the words this time. "Oh, God of the Bible . . ." He remembered her voice as having been rich and warm, but now it was laced with fear.

Then, in his dream, Dai watched in astonishment as the body of the girl was outlined by a golden glow. He could not turn his eyes away from her. Even her face appeared to change. In place of fear, he saw victory in her expression.

He looked to see if the dark and sinister figures that were approaching had grown closer, but they were still at a distance, only formless shapes, and he could not make out their appearance.

Just as he turned back to Sanara, Dai gasped, for now another figure had appeared in his dream.

The man—or perhaps it was an angel?—was dressed in a white robe with a cowl, but at times the garment changed into colors that flashed and glowed as he moved. Dai noticed that he had a golden trumpet hanging at his side.

Dai felt fear, one of the few times he had felt such an emotion, but the newcomer was so impressive looking that he could not blame himself.

And suddenly the man in white turned directly to Dai. "Dai Bando," he said, "Princess Sanara has been given an important mission by the God of heaven, and the enemy has sent one of his most wicked hordes against her."

In a dream, to be addressed by such a person did not seem strange. Instantly Dai cried out, "What can I do? What can I do to help her?"

At that point Dai snapped awake. He stared with

bewilderment around him. He was still so caught up in the dream that he scarcely knew where he was.

He stood and was aware that he was drenched with sweat. Absently he wiped his face as he realized something else—he could still see in his mind the face of Sanara. Her features were etched on his memory. He was astonished by this, but while he was pondering the weird dream, his attention was caught by the chime of an alarm. He looked down at his wristwatch and saw that it was time to meet with Raina.

Slowly he left the computer library, his mind filled with what he had just seen. Dai Bando asked himself aloud, "What did all that mean?"

5

The High Castle

The High Castle of Brutarius, suzerain of Capella, was impressive indeed. It was positioned a small distance from Mount Wildersarn, and that had the distinction of being the only mountain in the vast Central Plains of the largest continent on the planet. The castle had been built by the ancestors of Brutarius thousands of years ago when the tribal nations of Capella had not yet learned to live in peace.

Not ornate like some castles—those that had tall spires and were decorated with all forms of gargoyles—this castle was impressive for its strength and security. It appeared to be a single, huge granite rock, one-hundred-fifty feet high, one-hundred-fifty feet long, and one-hundred-fifty feet wide. In fact, it was a massive cube with doors and windows.

The castle itself had been built on a steep-sided, flat-topped mound. Giant turrets were constructed at the corners of the castle. These were connected by a fortified walkway that traveled the perimeter of the fortress. Surrounding the castle was an octagonal-shaped wall—called the inner wall—that was thirty feet high and had six fortified turrets. The gateway through the inner wall was the only place of entry to the High Castle.

An enormous outer wall stood at the bottom of the steep hill. More than seventy feet high and twenty feet across, this was the largest wall known to exist on all of Capella. The outer wall completely circled the hill, and it had eight fortified turrets. The stones used to construct this mighty barrier weighed several tons each. The gateway of the outer wall was itself a stone building that was almost as large as the castle, and battlements surrounded the top of the gatehouse.

Around the outer side of that wall was a deep, wide moat. Access to the massive steel doors of the outer gateway could be gained only by crossing the drawbridge that spanned the moat. Though the High Castle had been attacked many times by the warring tribal nations, no army had ever succeeded in penetrating that outer wall.

Looking out from any of the castle turrets, one could see the Great Central Plain. This was composed mostly of light green grasses with splotches of sage, and these spread out for miles in every direction—except in the direction of Mount Wildersarn. The mountain itself was exceedingly tall and was a refuge for many forms of wildlife. As the sun went down, Brutarius, his forehead furrowed with worry, sat alone in the tallest turret. It faced west toward Mount Wildersarn. The great mountain dwarfed the castle beneath his feet, he thought. His father had taught him that Mount Wildersarn had been sculpted by the Creator Himself to show man the awesome work of His hands.

Brutarius had been reflecting on something one of his most trusted servants had told him and his wife about a "King over all kings"—a heavenly King, who ruled over the affairs of the worldly kings. A King whose ways were unsearchable.

As he looked up at the stars that had begun to dot the heavens, Brutarius sighed deeply. Then he took one last look at the plain that lay before the castle—a plain blanketed by thousands of hideous creatures called "The Lo'custra."

The creatures had invaded Capella like a great swarm of locusts. Their bodies looked more like the insect called a praying mantis, except that they were much, much bigger. They were green and brown, similar to the coloring that dominated the Great Plain. And each creature was larger than a man. Their heads were chilling to look at. They were solid black, and the eyes were blood red. Large serrated teeth filled their lower jaws. These were able to quickly devour a grown man. Great sharp spines rose from the top of their heads.

The creatures appeared to be bent on only one purpose—the destruction of every living being on Capella. Thousands of Brutarius's mightiest warriors had already been slain. He bowed his head as he descended the stairs and thought, *If You are there, King of kings, we need Your help now!*

Brutarius started back to the war room and arrived in just a few minutes. There, he stood looking around the room at his few remaining generals. Most of his military leadership was missing from the chairs that surrounded the round council table. On the table lay a map that pinpointed the Lo'custra positions. It was obvious that the creatures had entirely surrounded the castle and would next attack the inner wall.

Brutarius sat down by the empty chair of his most gifted infantry general. "I can't believe Castor is dead," Brutarius whispered as he grasped the wooden arms of the chair. "I've never known a day without Castor at my side. And now . . ." He looked up at the tired faces of his men, many of whom bore serious injuries to their bodies.

Brutarius himself was not a tall man or muscular. His fair skin, blond hair, and blue eyes gave him a rather innocent appearance. He was wiry, however, and strong, and there was an air of command about him. He was, as all of the warriors around the table knew, a fierce fighter when necessary. He wore the dark green robe forbidden to all except the royal family of Capella.

From time to time he turned to gaze at Anmoir, his wife. A small woman, she also had fair hair and blue eyes and wore the royal green. She took no part outwardly in the council as Brutarius and his generals spoke of their great problem, but a worried look was in her eyes.

The commanding general of all the armed forces of Capella spoke up. "The problem is, Sire, the enemy is so greatly superior in numbers that they can overwhelm us in each battle just by sheer force."

The speaker was a tall, gray-haired man with a scar on his right cheekbone. Harvan was and looked every inch a fighter. His gray hair was clipped short, and he had sharp gray eyes that took in everything. He glanced around the table at the other officers and said, "They also care nothing for death. They willingly sacrifice themselves so that others can climb over them."

"That's true, I'm afraid, Your Majesty," said General Allo. He was a short, strong-looking man with reddish hair. His left hand was bandaged, and he looked pale, perhaps from loss of blood. "The situation, I fear, is quite serious. The enemy takes no captives, and they kill without mercy. On the Great Plain, as you know, they surrounded Castor and his army—one hundred thousand of our fiercest warriors. They attacked from virtually every direction, and many of our men were torn in two by these abominations at once. Then the Lo'custra quickly moved on to their next victims."

Allo swallowed down half his goblet of wine. "They have no regard even for each other. When we do succeed in wounding one of them, it is immediately consumed by its comrades!"

Then he continued his report. "The Lo'custra have sharp spikes that extend from the top of their heads. During the fighting at the outer gate, Colonel Pelon was impaled by one of them. Many of our men lost their lives in that way." Allo finished the goblet of wine and set it down on the table. "The news gets even worse. Reports say that several more of their space pods have landed on the Great Plain. Who knows how many more invaders have landed? All our communication lines have been severed. They devoured them too!"

"The problem is also our weapons." Commander Harvan frowned. "They have proved to be of little use against such creatures."

"What about hitting them with concentrated fire?" Brutarius asked. "There must be some way to stop them!"

"We've tried everything." General Allo groaned. "Large as they are, the Lo'custra move so swiftly that it's almost impossible to get a good shot."

"Very true, Your Majesty," Commander Harvan echoed. "Besides, our laser guns simply are not powerful enough. The creatures' armor deflects most of the blast."

The discussion went on for some time until, finally, the wife of Brutarius asked a question. "Do I hear you gentlemen saying that the only hope we have is for outside help?"

"I'm afraid that's true, my dear," Brutarius said, reaching over and taking her hand. There was certainly little hope in his face. "Unless the Galactic Command Star Fleet arrives in time, I'm afraid we have no alternative but to be destroyed."

"We would fight to the last man," Commander Harvan said.

"Yes," General Allo assured him grimly, "we would all do that."

"I do not doubt that you will all do your best," Brutarius said. And with that he indicated that the conference was over.

Commander Harvan arose and nodded at his officers. "Come, then. We will get to our posts. We will do our very best, Your Highness."

Brutarius watched as the soldiers left the room. Then he slumped back in his chair. He felt weary beyond belief, for the battle had drained him as it had the others. He looked over at his wife and said, "I think we had better send for Tramere."

"Is there no other way, my husband?"

"I'm afraid not. We can't risk waiting any longer." He rang a small bell beside his hand, and the door opened. When a servant entered, Brutarius said, "Summon Tramere."

"He is here, Sire. He has been waiting for your summons."

"Then, send him in."

"Yes, Sire."

The servant disappeared, and almost immediately the doorway appeared to be crowded. Actually only one man entered, but he was so enormous that he filled the entire door space.

Tramere was probably the largest man on Capella. His muscular limbs were like tree trunks. His skin was dark and hairy. His face, neck, and hands were covered with battle scars, and he wore a brightly colored turban that contrasted strangely with his rough appearance. The room seemed to tremble as he put his feet down firmly with each step and came to stand before the royal couple.

"Yes, Sire, what is your will?"

"Tramere, the hour grows dark for Capella. I am not at all certain that we will survive the attack of the Lo'custra."

"Let me go to the battle, Sire. I will show these beasts a thing or two!"

"I'm sure you would try, but these creatures are beyond human strength. Even beyond your strength, Tramere."

Tramere shook his head and scowled. "No, Sire, let me go! I will fight!"

Anmoir arose, and at once the big man knelt before her. But she still seemed small as a child in front of him. He had been devoted to her all of her life, and now he said, "What can I do for you, Your Majesty?"

"You can care for our daughter, Tramere," Anmoir said gently. She reached her hand out and touched his forehead in a royal gesture. "You have never failed us, and now you must do your best to see that she survives."

"Command me, Your Majesty. Whatever you say will be done."

Brutarius also arose and came to stand beside his wife. "You must take Sanara to Mount Wildersarn, Tramere. She will be safer there."

"And you can wait there with her for the arrival of the Galactic Command, Tramere."

"She will not want to go," the big man said, shaking his head. "She will want to remain here with you."

"She must leave if she is to survive," the suzerain said. "I will give you further instructions, but go prepare now for a long journey and a hard one. I would not send you to such a place by such a route as you will travel if it were not absolutely necessary. Get ready at once!"

As soon as the man had left the room, Anmoir turned to her husband and cried, "Brutarius, I do not think I can bear to be separated from Sanara!"

He put his arms around her. "Nor I, but it is what must be done. Let us go and speak with her."

Minutes later they were in the quarters of their daughter.

Sanara's room was spacious and had a large, open window that faced Mount Wildersarn. Located at one side of the room, the bed was adorned with a golden satin comforter. Large pillows made of the same material were stacked three high against the wooden headboard. The walls were decorated with gold-and-white coverings.

Everywhere one looked were displays of gifts that had been given to Sanara from the people of Capella over the last sixteen years. It didn't matter if the gifts were plain or fancy, Sanara obviously cherished each one. Her mother had occasionally suggested that they box up some of the gifts and store them, but Sanara always refused.

Sanara was surprised to see her parents and got up at once. "Is something wrong?" she said, reaching out to them.

Each of them took a hand and held it firmly, and it was Brutarius who said, "We are going to send you away to a safe place, Sanara."

"No, I want to stay with you!"

"We knew that you would say that." Brutarius smiled. "You have the courage of the royal house, but going away is truly necessary."

"You must leave if you are to survive," her mother

said. She took Sanara's hand with both of hers. "You will be the one to help our people survive."

"Yes, your mother and I must stay and fight," the suzerain said. "Otherwise, the people will lose heart, and all will surely be lost."

"But I *can't* leave you!"

Brutarius shook his head. "I must ask you to give me your sacred word that you will go. I know this is difficult for you. It is for us. But it is for your own safety, and we must also think of Capella. There must be a ruler here to rally the people in the future."

Finally Sanara, her face full of sadness, gave her word that she would leave.

And then her father said, "And, Sanara, you must leave quickly. I do not know how long we can hold out."

Tramere was waiting in the council room when Brutarius, Anmoir, and Sanara arrived. The big man came at once to stand beside the princess. He smiled down at her. His face was not a handsome face, but his smile was warm. "Do not worry, Princess, I will keep you safe."

"I know you will do that, Tramere."

The perimeter of the war room was built with many cabinets that contained artifacts and royal documents of historical importance to Capella. Brutarius reached behind one of the cabinets, and his fingers found a secret button. He pressed it.

Two of the built-in cabinets immediately swung open, exposing a door. In less than two seconds, the secret door rolled back into the wall.

"I never knew that was there!" Sanara exclaimed.

"No, nor did anyone else except myself and your mother."

Moving closer, Tramere stooped and looked into the dark passageway. "Where does it lead to?"

Brutarius explained quickly. "This passage leads to a man-made tunnel that travels many miles—all the way to the mountain—and I have no idea who dug such a thing. One of our family, no doubt. Perhaps one of the rulers, back in ancient times, planned a way to escape if the High Castle fell."

Brutarius turned then and went to his desk, where he shuffled through some papers. He came back with a leather case, which he opened, and brought out a parchment yellow with age.

"Guard this with your life, Tramere. It can mean life or death to you."

"What is it, Father?"

"It is a map of the tunnel system." He spread out the map on the table. "You will see here," he said, pointing, "that there are many tunnels leading off to the side. Follow this map closely, or both of you could perish."

"Have you followed this passageway yourself, Sire?" Tramere asked curiously.

"Yes, once when I was a very young man. My father revealed it to me, and I took the map and went all the way to Mount Wildersarn. I recall that I nearly got lost several times, so you must be very careful."

"Do we emerge from the tunnel close to Wildersarn?" Sanara asked.

"You do, and then you will follow a trail to the top of the mountain."

"Provisions have been stored up there in a cabin, my dear," Anmoir said. "We have seen to that. You will be safe until . . ." She could not finish her sentence.

Sanara went to her mother. Her eyes were filled with tears, and she said, "Mother, let me stay with you. Please."

"We've already explained that, dear. You must go. For your sake and for Capella's."

For some time Sanara struggled with her tears, but she seemed to understand that there was no other sensible choice. She kissed each of her parents and then said, "All right, Tramere. I'm ready."

"Go with the King of kings, my darling," Anmoir said, giving her one more embrace.

Brutarius then held her tightly for a moment and said huskily, "May the King over all kings be with you, indeed."

The king put a powerful torch into Tramere's hand, and the big man, followed by Sanara, entered the dark passage. He had to stoop to get his massive body through the entrance.

Then Brutarius touched the secret button, and the door closed behind them. Turning to his wife, he said huskily, "Now it is all in the hands of Tramere's God."

"Yes, my dear, and we will trust Him to keep her safe and to deliver our planet!"

6

Truth in Tunnels

Zeno Thrax, first officer of the *Daystar*, looked down mournfully at his plate.

"I wish I had some mushrooms," he said.

Captain Edge, seated next to him, looked up. "Mushrooms?" he exclaimed. "Why, the cook can probably find some mushrooms if you ask for them."

"No, I mean mushrooms from Mentor Seven." Thrax, a perfect albino, ran his hand over his white hair. His colorless eyes always gleamed whenever he remembered his native home.

On Mentor Seven everyone lived underground, and Edge knew that at times his first officer grew a little lonely for the dark tunnels and caverns where he had been born and where he had lived throughout his early youth. It had been quite a leap from those tunnels, so dark and dreary, into the outer reaches of space.

Thrax shook his shoulders and said wistfully, "They just don't grow mushrooms anywhere else like they do back on my home planet."

The two men continued to eat their lunch, and Edge started to talk about their mission.

"I wouldn't admit this to anyone else, Zeno, but I wish it was your planet we were headed to right now."

"Captain, if you were to land this ship on Mentor Seven, they would use our bodies to fertilize the very mushrooms I just mentioned."

"You're right, of course," Edge admitted. "Well . . ." He took another bite of something that looked like sauerkraut and eggplant mixed together. The messy-looking vegetable was called "ploin," and it was very spicy. It was native to the planet Dernof, the same planet that supplied the Intergalactic fleet with fine oxen leather for its furniture. Between bites, the captain said, "I never could understand why your people are so unsociable, Zeno."

"I share those feelings with you. Prejudice can run deep into the fabric of any people." The albino looked at him with pale eyes showing no emotion at all.

Thoughtfully, Mark Edge looked beyond Thrax and through the ports that lined the chow hall bulkhead. The *Daystar* was cruising in Star Drive. The star field appeared to be floating past the ship, but Captain Edge knew this was only the visual effect Star Drive played on the eyes. He stared out into empty space, then took another bite of ploin.

"Zeno, how are the long-range scans coming?"

"I've had Heck and Bronwen working on them. And it looks like Heck first spotted the Lo'custra space vessels as we were winding down our last mission."

"What do you mean?" Edge frowned. "He never *reported* seeing anything unusual."

"Heck was trying to impress Olga Von Kemp at the time."

"Just between me and you, Cadet Von Kemp doesn't appear to be Heck's type." Edge chuckled and took a sip of milk.

Zeno looked at the captain questioningly.

"I mean she's . . . well . . . she needs to loosen up just a little. Von Kemp's so serious, she makes me uncomfortable. When I'm around her, it's like she's looking over my shoulder all the time." Edge patted Zeno on the arm. "Anyway, finish what you were saying."

"While Heck was showing off his new long-range

sensors to Von Kemp, he picked up on the Lo'custra ships—or whatever they are. According to the scans, each was as large as a Magnum Deep Space Cruiser."

"Then—but why wasn't all that on his report?"

"For one thing, Heck had his charm turned on. He's a real knucklehead when that happens. Second, the data stated that the ships were made of some sort of dense resin material and had no form of propulsion. Altogether, there were about one hundred fifty of the things. *Pods* are what I think they really are. Besides, except for maybe twenty of them, they were headed out of our galaxy."

"And where were the twenty pods headed, if I may ask?"

"Unfortunately, according to Heck's data they were headed toward the star Algol—."

"And, in particular, for the planet Capella," Edge finished for him.

"I'm afraid so."

"What's frightening," Edge said—he shoved back his plate and picked up the milk goblet—"is that there are no records of anyone having seen the Lo'custra close up and living to tell about it. There are nasty rumors about them, though."

"What sort of rumors, sir?"

"Rumors dating back for thousands of years. On inhabited planets on the fringes of the galaxy there are records of large meteor-like masses falling out of the heavens. They really weren't meteors, though. The friction of the air caused the—pods?—to burn as bright as meteors. After landing, the things split open, and hordes of Lo'custra warriors emerged. Their attack was always so swift and devastating that all human life was destroyed on the planet in a short time. By the time rescue ships arrived, the Lo'custra and their pods were gone."

Zeno followed the line of logic. "But if the pods have no propulsion system, how did they get off the planet?" he asked.

"That remains a mystery to our science. We know so little about them, anyway. No picture or description has been discovered. In fact, the only reason they are called Lo'custra is because someone wrote the word on a wall with his own blood, apparently just before he died."

"And why call them that?" Zeno puzzled. "When was the last invasion?"

"The last one that Intergalactic Command knows about was over a thousand years ago. They appear to usually just dwell in space between galaxies, but that's only a guess."

"And our mission is to go to Capella—into harm's way! I think I've changed my mind! Let's go to Mentor Seven instead."

Edge reflected on Zeno's comment. He couldn't decide which would be worse, although the known was somehow more comfortable than the unknown. Finally the captain said, "Well, first we've got to do something for Commandant Lee. I want you to formulate a plan that will allow us to scout the planet without being discovered, Zeno."

"Yes sir, I'll get on it at once."

"Good. You always do a fine job on plans like this."

Captain Edge stood and reached down for his glass. He finished drinking the milk in it, then put the goblet back and picked up the tray. He was about to take the tray back to the counter when he caught a glimpse of something that made him flinch. It was only a black blur, but he yelled automatically, "Contessa, get away!"

Unfortunately Captain Edge's reflexes were not as quick as those of the super German shepherd. Her full weight struck him, knocking him to the floor.

"Not again!" he yelled. Some of the remaining ploin sloshed over his face, and before he could free himself, Contessa was licking it off.

Jerusha came into the chow hall just in time to hear Edge's yells, and she dashed over to where Contessa was keeping her captain pinned down. Edge was calling the dog and her ancestors a variety of nasty names.

Jerusha tried not to smile—she even managed a worried look, for this sort of thing had happened more than once before. "Come on, Contessa, get off the captain!" She seized the dog by the scruff and dragged her away. "Shame on you. Bad dog! Bad dog!"

Struggling to his feet, Capt. Mark Edge did not look particularly like a role model for a captain of a space cruiser. Spilled ploin was all over his tunic, although Contessa had licked most of it from his face. He glanced around furiously at the off-duty members of the crew, who also were trying to hide their smiles. He yelled, "You'll pay for this, dog. You'll pay!"

Then he almost slipped on the tray and lost whatever little dignity he had left. He glared down at the huge black dog. "I'm going to feed you to the Lo'custra —that's what I'm going to do!" he threatened.

The captain had no sooner left the chow hall than he heard laughter following him, and a storm cloud darkened his features. "Blast that animal! I *would* like to feed her to the Lo'custra. But I suppose I won't."

Raina St. Clair had entered the chow hall just in time to see the scene between Contessa and Captain Edge. She wisely stayed back out of the way, and as soon as he left—raging about what he was going to do to the worthless dog—she went to a small table somewhat isolated from the others. Her shipmates were nearby but not too close.

She didn't want to appear obvious. The table she had chosen was near one of the ports providing a fine view of a nearby nebula. It was purple with splashes of white spoking out from the center. The display resembled an orchid, except that this orchid was five light-years across. Its purple light illuminated the table in front of her. To Raina, the nebula provided a romantic setting.

Seating herself, she glanced over at another porthole, where her image was reflected. She wondered if she had made the right choice about her clothes. Pulling out a small purse, she studied her face and then applied some lipstick.

"Hey, doll, what's happening?"

Glancing up, Raina saw with dismay that Heck Jordan, his tray piled high with food, was standing beside her table. *Oh, no,* she thought, *not Heck!* She really liked the overweight boy, and her liking was mingled with concern, for he was not a Christian. But of all times, she did not want him at her table just now.

Heck seemed not to notice the look on Raina's face. He sat down and placed his tray before him. Then he began unloading it, which was quite a chore because, as usual, gluttony had gotten the best of him. He had piled his plate high with ploin and strips of meat called mosumi, which came from the planet Zonair. Mosumi was a lizardlike creature. Its meat tasted best when it had been roasted on small strips of wood. The wood was burned on either end, giving the meat a flavor similar to mesquite. The taste was like roast chicken with a hint of ham.

When the tray was emptied, he began to eat, at the same time boasting about how much work he had done at his computer that afternoon.

Raina sat helplessly, glancing from time to time at the two entryways and hoping that Heck would finish eating quickly and leave.

"I'll tell you what, doll. After I get through eating, suppose we go up to the observation lounge? Me and you can look at the stars, and who knows what will happen, hey?"

"I really don't think—"

"Hey, there's old Dai Bando. I hope he leaves us alone. That guy's a pest, you know?"

Raina's heart sank. She looked up to see Dai Bando entering from the rear entrance. When he gave her a wave, she jumped to her feet and said, "Excuse me, Heck—I have to speak to Dai."

"Aw, what do you want to fool with him for? He's a loser."

Ignoring Heck's complaint, Raina quickly crossed the chow hall. She moved too quickly, in fact. When she reached the spot where Captain Edge had lost his tray under the attack of Contessa, her foot encountered a slippery spot. She felt her feet flying out from under her.

It was one of those times when Raina's mind worked more rapidly than her body. She flung out her arms, but her mind was already crying, *Oh no, I'm going to fall flat and look like an utter idiot to Dai!*

Dai Bando had been still six or seven feet away when Raina suddenly began to lose her balance. But by the time her feet went out from under her and she was airborne, heading for the floor, he had leaped forward with a burst of that amazing, almost superhuman, speed and reflex he possessed that no one could ever explain. He reached her, somehow his arms shot out under her knees and her arms, and he swooped her up.

Raina was totally confused. It had all happened so fast. One minute she had been headed for the floor to make a spectacle out of herself. The next, Dai was lightly holding her and replacing her feet carefully on the floor.

"Are you all right?" he asked.

Raina found that her heart was pounding. She could only nod and whisper, "Yes."

He gave her a friendly smile. "All right?" he asked again. He looked as though he was afraid she would fall.

"I–I still feel a little bit wobbly. I'm not like you, Dai. I don't have a lot of stamina."

Dai took her arm, and a worried look came into his eyes. "Maybe you need to go lie down."

"Oh no," Raina said quickly. "I'm not that bad off. It just frightened me a little bit."

"Well, you'd better sit down, anyway. You do look a little pale."

If she was pale, Raina knew it was not the fall. She had had dreams of Dai Bando that she had never revealed to a single soul, and now here they were. He had held her! He was even now holding her arm! They were together!

"Let's just take a little walk—if you don't mind—unless you're hungry," she said quickly, seeing that Heck was starting to emerge from behind his mountain of food and was looking at them as if he might come over.

"That would be fine. Suppose we go to the port up forward?"

"I'd like that very much."

The pressure of his hand gave Raina a warm, comforted feeling, and as they arrived at the forward port, where the stars were all laid out before them, she whispered, "I wish I were as strong as you, Dai."

"Here, sit down. And what you said—that's what I want to talk to you about."

He seated her on the blue leather-covered bench

that faced the large observation window. She could still see the purple orchid nebula from this observation port, although the Star Drive engines had increased their distance from it, making the nebula appear much smaller now.

The stars stood out like glittering diamonds on the ebony blackness of space, and when Dai sat down beside her on the bench, Raina thought, *There couldn't be a more romantic setting than this.* She waited breathlessly to hear what he would say.

"I don't think it's a big thing to be strong physically," he began. "There's another kind of strength that I think is more important."

Raina was so flustered by his closeness that she could only say, "Is that right?" in a meaningless way.

"Well, sure. What good does it do just to be physically strong?"

"Well, it saved Jerusha's life and mine too. More than once it's been your strength and speed that's saved the Rangers, Dai."

"Maybe so, but there's a kind of problem that physical strength won't do anything for." He seemed to be waiting for her to respond. When she didn't, he said, "You know, there's such a thing as spiritual warfare."

"Spiritual warfare," she repeated stupidly. He wanted to talk about spiritual warfare.

"You know—when we have trouble in the spiritual realm. I've talked to Aunt Bronwen about it a lot, but I'd like to discuss it with someone my own age. Like you."

Suddenly Raina blinked hard. "You wanted to meet with me to talk about spiritual warfare?"

"Yes. Is that all right?"

Ordinarily Raina would have been eager to talk to anyone about the things of the Lord. But this time, all she felt was a stab of disappointment.

She thought, *I was hoping he wanted to talk to me about—well, about me as a person!*

The disappointment grew in Raina as he began talking about the problems he saw in his Christian life. She drew back, folded her arms, and listened, but she could not enter into what he was saying. *I thought he might—I thought he might like me the way a boy likes a girl, but he just sees me as somebody to talk to about the Bible!*

Abruptly Raina got up and said, "Dai, I'm not feeling too well." This was not a lie. Although she felt well physically now, she felt miserable inside, as miserable and disappointed as if she had lost something.

Dai rose at once. "Oh, I'm sorry!" he said. "I should have known. We can talk about it later."

And Raina hurried from the room.

Raina had no sooner gone than Heck came up with an enormous candy bar in his hand. He took a bite and, chewing vigorously, mumbled around it. "Boy, didn't Raina look great tonight? She was dressed to the hilt."

But Dai was looking out the port and wondering, *Did I say something wrong? I'm always doing something I shouldn't. She looked disturbed. I wonder what it was.*

Heck stuffed another great bite of candy bar into his cheek. Now he looked like a chipmunk with both cheeks full. He could hardly speak, but he managed to say, "You know, Dai, when I hit it rich, Raina won't be interested in you. She'll have eyes only for me."

Dai barely heard him, though. Suddenly, as he looked out into the darkness of space, he had a startling flash of clear memory.

For the moment, he forgot the *Daystar*, he forgot Raina, he even forgot Heck, standing behind him chewing candy. Dai was seeing again the face in his dream, the face of Sanara. It was as clear as anything he had ever seen, and then slowly it faded. He turned from the port and said in a tight voice, "You know, Heck, destiny can be a funny thing." Without another word he turned and left Heck staring and mystified.

"What do you mean by that—destiny can be a funny thing?" Heck called after him. Destiny's getting rich, that's what it is."

Dai strode purposefully along the main corridor until he saw Contessa. The dog trotted up to him at once, and he knelt beside her and put his arms around her. He whispered, "Contessa, you're the only female on this ship that understands me. Come on, let's go get something to eat."

Contessa wagged her tail enthusiastically, barked twice, and then they headed for the chow hall.

Several times Sanara and Tramere almost made wrong turns. They found the maze of tunnels confusing to say the least. Twice they had halted and stared at length at the map until agreeing that they had made a mistake.

Now, after three hours of steady walking, they came to be what appeared to be a Y in the passageway.

"I can't tell from the map which fork we should take," Sanara's protector admitted as he turned the map around in different directions.

"Which one *do* we take, the right or the left?" Sanara asked.

She was bone tired, and there was something frightening about the tunnel itself. There were bats for one thing, and from time to time they had come gibbering and squeaking by her face. Each time, she beat them off, and they disappeared into what apparently were air holes that led to the surface.

"Let's look at the map again," Tramere said. They studied the map together, and at last he said, "I would say the right one is the way to go."

"I'll be glad when we get out of this," Sanara said wearily. "Give me the torch."

Sanara reached for the flashlight, but Tramere said, "No, let me always go first. We don't know what's in there."

"All right, Tramere. Whatever you say."

Tramere started forward again. But even as he rounded the new turn, he hesitated as though some slight sound had caught his attention. Tramere might have been big, but he had tremendously fast reflexes. He flung himself back, knocking Sanara to the floor and yelling, *"Look out!"*

Sanara caught a glimpse of something that flashed. And when they got to their feet, she saw that a giant ax blade had swung out from a hidden spot in the wall.

Fear sent a chill up her spine. "How do we know that there aren't more of those, Tramere? The map doesn't indicate anything about ax blades, and Father didn't mention it, but . . ."

"Your father may not have known," Tramere said solemnly. "We'll just have to be very careful and go slowly. No telling what's ahead of us."

"No, but I suppose we'd better go on."

"We'll stop and eat in another hour. Here—have something to drink."

"Thank you, Tramere." Sanara drank from the juice bottle that the giant handed her. When he had taken a drink himself, she said, "Let's go on. Quickly."

The two continued their journey, and at one point Sanara said, "You know, you make me feel very safe, Tramere."

"I wouldn't have been much help if that ax had cut my head off. I was careless."

"But it didn't. And you weren't careless. Tell me something about your home."

"My home? I haven't thought much about home lately."

"What sort of a place is it?"

Tramere thought for a time, then said, "Well, for one thing it's a place where they follow the teachings of Jesus Christ."

For some time as they moved down the dark corridor, here and there making turns, frequently stopping to study the map, Tramere told Sanara about the teachings of Jesus.

Then he said, "My family left our home world when I was a teenager, and we crash-landed on Capella. We were all captured by the Fenians, and they made slaves out of us."

"Oh, how awful!"

"Yes, it is awful. I'm glad your family doesn't practice slavery."

"How did you come to meet my father and mother, then? How did you come to get away from the Fenians?"

"Well, my parents died, and I had gotten so big and strong that I found a way to escape. Believe it or not, I wound up in the wilderness of Mount Wildersarn, where we are headed now." He stopped and looked down at her, and she could see by the light that illuminated his face that he was smiling. "You'll be interested in this. I saw a Tybern snow cat there."

Pound for pound, the solid white snow cat was the most fierce animal on Capella. Its average length was eight feet. Its canine teeth were six inches long and razor sharp. Having oversized paws, the cat was able to slay its victims with one pass of its claws. The Tybern snow cat was a loner except during mating season. People could hear their cries many miles away from Mount Wildersarn.

"The snow cat I saw was stalking a man who didn't see him. Just as the cat leaped, I was able to get to him. I broke the cat's neck with one blow from behind and saved the man's life."

"I'll bet he was both grateful and surprised."

"You know him well." Tramere grinned.

"*I* know him? Who was it, Tramere?"

"It was your father."

"You saved his life? I never knew that!"

"Well, it's been kind of a secret between us. In any case, I've been his bodyguard ever since."

"Father loves you very much, but I never understood why," Sanara said quietly.

"He is a great man. He treats me as a friend instead of a servant. And now I'm your protector."

"That's wonderful!" She reached out her hand, and he took it in his massive grip.

"Who will protect you while you're protecting me?"

Tramere said quietly, holding her hand firmly, "Whether I live or die is of no concern, for my trust is in God. My only prayer now is that my princess and my master and his family will all survive."

"Thank you, Tramere."

The two walked on, and ten minutes later they saw sunlight ahead. They had reached the mouth of the tunnel.

"There, Tramere! We are safe." She turned to him and said, "You've fulfilled your task."

"Not yet," Tramere said. "Not until we get to the top of Mount Wildersarn!"

7
The Mountain Trail

The *Daystar* circled the planet Capella at a relatively slow speed. Captain Edge and his first officer and friend, Zeno Thrax, stood before their scanners, examining the data that was coming in. Darting from cloud cover to cloud cover, the *Daystar* had apparently remained hidden from the eyes of the Lo'custra. So far, the creatures seemed completely oblivious to the ship and its scanners.

The instruments revealed that fourteen of the twenty or so "pods" had crash-landed on Capellan soil without damage. The huge vessels were like dark brown insect cocoons—upon landing, each pod had split open, allowing its inhabitants to race in all directions.

Zeno double-checked his scanner. "Captain, there is no discernible chain of command. The Lo'custra creatures are simply swarming over the planet like giant locusts. Their bodies are different from a locust's, though—they resemble a praying mantis more. But they are very quick." Zeno fine-tuned a couple of switches. "Want to hear what they sound like?"

As Thrax turned on the bridge speaker, the shrill sound of "*Lo-cus-tra*" filled the air. He examined more data. "The sound is produced by their legs rubbing against their thorax when they run."

The captain was standing beside Zeno with his arms crossed. "Those poor people," he said. "Just imagine hearing a swarm of these guys running at you!"

"They appear to have at least some sort of rudimentary intelligence, sir, but so far I haven't discovered how they communicate. From this far up, they act like swarming ants more than anything else." Zeno sat back in his chair. "I remember Bronwen telling me there is something in the Bible about a plague of locusts. They devoured everything in their path." Then Zeno looked right at Captain Edge. "I think these things are insects, Captain!"

"Insects!" Mark Edge looked at him incredulously.

"I don't pretend to understand the mechanics of their form of space travel," Thrax said, "but my guess is that the Lo'custra are a form of space insect. From time to time, maybe the hive sends out a detachment of pods to stock up on food. Then the pods return to the main group with the newly acquired supplies. Twenty pods would make twenty storehouses of food for the rest of the colony. That's my guess."

Edge frowned down at the scanner. "Looks to me like some of them are performing some work on that pod there." He pointed.

"Let me see," Zeno said. After reviewing the data, his eyes widened. "Well, what do you know! They *are* working! They're repairing the damaged pods!" He adjusted another scanner. "Something appears to be coming from their mouths—maybe a kind of resin?—and they use it to close the seams back up. Remarkable!" But then Zeno Thrax sat up straight. "Look, Captain! Look at all those Lo'custra there—racing toward the High Castle."

"Yes, I see them, First." Captain Edge's eyes narrowed, and a frown creased his forehead. "They certainly brought enough of them, didn't they?"

"They certainly did, and it appears they have enough insect power to overwhelm the Capellans unless something happens." A pale fire suddenly glowed in his colorless eyes, brightening them. He asked almost eagerly, "Shall I call for battle stations?"

"No, not yet, Zeno. We have to be cautious. We don't know what we're getting into here."

The two officers studied the Lo'custran pods resting on the Great Plain of Capella. They kept watching the contingent advancing toward the castle.

"It's apparent that these poor people don't have a chance, Captain," Thrax murmured. "Are you certain we don't want to leap into the fight?"

"Nothing I'd like better, but that's not what we were ordered to do. If we get ourselves killed, we wouldn't be able to transmit any information to Commander Lee and the rescue force that's coming."

Thrax continued to watch, then said, "You know what? I was watching some old motion pictures not long ago. They depicted a part of Earth's history when Indians would surround what they called a wagon train."

"I saw some of those when I was younger, myself. The defenders always drew their wagons around in a circle."

"That's right, and then the attackers would ride their horses around the circle, shooting arrows into the wagons." Thrax motioned with his head to the planet below. "That's more or less what's happening here, isn't it, Captain? The Lo'custra are surrounding the castle."

"I suppose it is. And if help doesn't arrive pretty soon, these defenders are going to be all wiped out."

"The motion picture I was watching had a man in it called John Wayne, a big fellow. He led mounted soldiers to the rescue."

The creases on Edge's forehead deepened. "Well, I wish John Wayne—or, better still, Commandant Winona Lee—would get here with the rescue party right away."

At that moment Jerusha and Dai hurried onto the bridge.

"Captain," Dai said breathlessly, "can I speak with you, sir?"

Dai was usually a calm young man. It was uncommon to see him shaken by anything. Exchanging glances with his first officer, Edge said quickly, "What is it, Dai? Something gone wrong?"

Dai hesitated, as though debating with himself whether to tell the captain his news.

"Well, speak up, Bando. What is it?" Edge said rather impatiently.

Dai cast a desperate glance at Jerusha, who nodded encouragingly. "Go ahead, Dai," she said. "Tell the captain what you told me."

Swallowing hard, Dai Bando said, "Captain, I know you don't believe much in dreams and things like that, but I've had a dream . . ."

"A *dream?* What kind of a dream?"

Dai quickly described a vivid dream that he had had—a dream about a frightened girl and her pursuers. When he had finished, he pointed to the mountain that sat below them in the middle of a great plain, and he said, "And that's it right there, sir. That mountain is the one I saw in my dream."

Staring down at the peak, Edge was confused for a moment, although he did not allow it to show on his face. A starship captain must never show indecision, but right at that moment that was exactly what he felt.

"I've had only three dreams like that in my life, sir, and the other two turned out to be real. Truly, it was quite different from an ordinary dream."

How am I supposed to handle this one? Edge thought. *I don't believe in getting messages by way of dreams. But stranger things have happened. Besides, one thing in Dai's dream* was *real—that mountain, which none of us have seen before now.*

Nothing else came to his mind, so he fixed his eyes on Dai Bando and said, "And you think that girl you saw is real and that she's in trouble?"

"I think so, sir."

"What do you think, First?"

Zeno Thrax always said he was not a man who dreamed a great deal himself. But he had tremendous confidence in their navigator, Bronwen Llewellen. He'd once told Edge that he'd never known a woman like her and that her insight into the nature of things was more than natural. And he'd also told the captain that he thought this young man had similar qualities.

So Edge was not greatly surprised when the first officer said, "I think we had better proceed on the basis that the dream that Dai Bando had is valid."

Captain Edge then surprised himself by saying, "Very well. In that case, set a course for that mountain down there." He looked toward the viewer screen that displayed a map of Capella. "What *is* that mountain? Does it have a name?"

"Yes, according to the map, it's called Mount Wildersarn."

Edge hit the transmitter on his belt and ordered, "Lieutenant Jaleel, prepare a recon party."

Instantly Jaleel's voice came back, "Aye, aye, sir!"

"Now, land the ship, First, while I go over this dream again with this young man."

As Captain Edge listened to Dai Bando recount his dream again, Zeno Thrax carefully maneuvered the *Daystar*. He lowered the cruiser until it came to rest on a stony ledge located on the opposite side of the mountain from the High Castle.

"Scanners are picking up several Lo'custra poking

around at the base of the mountain," Thrax advised Edge. "But if they're aware of us, they show no signs of it."

"Good!" Edge glanced over at Dai Bando. "Maybe that will give us the time we need."

Carefully Tramere edged toward the circle of light that marked the end of the tunnel. He had drawn the massive sword he carried, a weapon larger than the ordinary blade and so heavy it was capable of cutting through most body armor. He held it tightly, and his dark eyes moved from side to side as they reached the tunnel opening.

"Be careful, Princess," he muttered. "I don't want us to be seen."

Sanara carefully crept forward until she stood in the shadow of the giant. Looking down the mountainside, she drew in her breath suddenly. "Look, Tramere. Isn't that a Lo'custra camp?"

"Yes, and I don't like the looks of it."

"Well, they can't *hear* us from here. And if we're going to the top, at least we're ahead of them."

"But we don't know that they haven't sent scouts on ahead," Tramere argued. He bit his lower lip, considering. Finally he shrugged his burly shoulders. "Well, there's nothing for it. We'll just have to be very careful."

"Do you know the way from here, Tramere?" Sanara asked, glancing up the mountainside now. She saw a faint trail there, but it was overgrown with bush and brambles and looked little used. "Is that the pathway?"

"That's one of them," Tramere answered. "What we'll have to do is to travel as quietly as we can and keep out of sight. If they spot us, it won't be good."

"You lead the way, and I'll stay right behind you."

"All right, but climbing won't be pleasant. Look at those thorns and briars. My own skin can take it, but you are likely to be scratched."

Sanara had worn a fine leather jacket. She had rolled up the sleeves, but now she rolled them down, saying, "This jacket will protect me a little."

"All right, let's go."

The two emerged cautiously from the tunnel and stealthily began their ascent to the top of Mount Wildersarn. It was hard going, as Tramere had said. The vines, branches, and thorns seemed to reach out and grab them. They had not traveled far before Sanara's jacket was badly scarred by the briars, but she made no complaint.

For some time they climbed, as quietly as possible, through the brush, thankful for the trees that shielded their movements from the camp below. Sanara had no trouble moving very quietly, but Tramere was so large and his feet so heavy that he could not go noiselessly.

Sanara once thought, *This is like following a big elephant.* She was amused for the moment but quickly grew serious again. She knew that their lives were on a razor's edge. She had learned enough about the invaders to know that, if they were captured, they would be killed immediately. The Lo'custra took no prisoners.

"Wait!" Tramere suddenly warned, his voice a mere whisper.

Sanara stopped at once and looked around her huge bodyguard. Just ahead of them, fewer than fifty yards away, was a lone Lo'custra, the first that she had ever seen up close.

"Just the sight of it is awful—it's like something

out of a horrible nightmare!" Sanara said in a whisper as she crouched behind a large gray rock.

Tramere found a larger rock to hide behind. And then from his hiding place he threw a small pebble at Sanara to attract her attention.

When she looked at him, he pointed. A Tybern snow cat was perched on a ledge above the Lo'custra. But when the cat attempted to leap onto the Lo'custra's back, the creature shifted its position in a split second. It had been a trap. The snow-white cat screeched in horror. And the alien creature then shook the dead cat to the ground.

Sanara turned away and buried her face in her arms. She had never seen such brutality. To stay safe, she and Tramere must not make a sound.

Cautiously, she joined him, and they watched the Lo'custra devour the snow cat. But then, suddenly, another movement caught Sanara's eye, and she touched Tramere on the arm to get his attention.

He looked at her in surprise, then followed with his eyes the gesture she made. Down in the ravine, a second Tybern snow cat was sniffing the body of a dead farcel. The farcel was a clever hunter, resembling an Earth otter but with long canines and a poison barb on its tail. Sanara knew that usually they hunted in packs.

Her thoughts turned back to their situation. She and Tramere could not go back, and they could not pass by the Lo'custra without being seen. To Sanara it felt like hours before the creature completed his messy meal. Her nerves grew tense from waiting, but finally the Lo'custra raised himself and looked around. Then—moving more quickly than she had thought possible—he made his way down to the bottom of the ravine and disappeared.

"Come—let's get to the top before we run into more of those monsters!" Tramere urged.

They started up the mountain trail but suddenly stopped again when a hideous cry rent the air.

"What *was* that?" Sanara gasped, her face pale.

"I think it was the snow cat in the ravine. It must have gotten caught by that Lo'custra. Anything that can kill snow cats that easily, we don't want to fool with. Come."

They still seemed miles away from the peak, and Tramere finally estimated, "We'll be lucky to get to the top before dark." He looked at her, calculation in his dark eyes. "I don't know if you can make it, Princess."

"Don't worry about me. You go ahead. I'll follow."

"All right, but let me know if you can't go any farther, and I'll carry you."

Tramere plunged ahead. They climbed around or over huge rocks, and from time to time the path closed entirely, thick with briars and vines that grasped at them. Tramere cleared the worst of it out of the way with his sword, making it easier for Sanara.

"I hope there's plenty to eat in that hut," he growled. "We'll be starved by the time we get there."

On and on they tramped, stopping only to rest for brief periods. Sanara was a healthy young woman with a strong, athletic form. She was far more agile than Tramere, and actually by the time they had traveled several hours she was fresher than he was. Once, she even started around him and lightly ran ahead into an open space.

But her protector called out at once, "Princess, don't do that!"

"It's all right, Tramere," Sanara said. "There's no one here."

"We don't know what's here!" Tramere growled. "You let me go first. If anybody's going to get killed on this trip to the top, I want it to be me and not you!"

8
The *Daystar* Lands

The *Daystar* touched down just as evening fell. The landing was so expertly carried out that it hardly jarred the ship as it came to rest on the rock outcropping.

Then the exit door slid into the hull, and Captain Edge came down the walkway. He was followed closely by Lt. Tara Jaleel. Both of them kept their eyes moving from side to side, alert for any signs of the enemy.

Tara Jaleel was almost as tall as the captain. She was a descendant of an old tribe of African warriors, the Masai, who had the reputation of once being the fiercest warriors on Earth. She walked along, taking long strides, her fierce dark eyes never stopping, her lips drawn together in a line. She was a rather attractive woman in spite of her fierce features, and she loved nothing better than battle.

"I think we're almost exactly on the opposite side of Mount Wildersarn from the High Castle," Edge said. "But I'm not sure of what we'll find here. We could run into a Lo'custran patrol at any minute."

"I wish we would. I'd like to find out something about these Lo'custra. From what I've heard—" Jaleel nodded almost with approval "—they'd be fine adversaries in battle."

Curiously, Edge looked at the tall woman beside him. He never felt quite comfortable with Lieutenant Jaleel. She seemed to have none of the so-called finer aspects of womanhood—gentleness, tenderness, love. Now, despite the urgency of the moment, he asked impulsively, "Do you ever think of anything but fighting, Tara?"

Surprised by the question, Tara Jaleel stopped and faced the captain. "What do you mean, sir?"

"Well . . . I mean, most women want a home, and family, and children. Things like that. I've never heard you one time mention any desire along those lines."

The question seemed disturbing to Lieutenant Jaleel. Perhaps she had indeed known those impulses but had kept them buried beneath her fierce demeanor. "I am the battle officer on board a star cruiser. This is no time to be thinking about a nursery and bottles and changing diapers!" she snapped.

Edge saw that he had opened a subject that was unpleasant to his lieutenant, and he retreated at once. "Well, I just wondered," he said, then abruptly changed the subject. "Look at these prints in the ground, Jaleel."

"One set of prints resembles those of a large dog. The animal that made them must be six feet long," the lieutenant estimated. She looked at another set of tracks that accompanied the first. They were much larger. "Now, these tracks look formidable. They must be from some kind of giant cat." She looked fiercely at the captain. "But none of this is anything I can't handle."

Captain Edge pointed, indicating the direction the animals had taken. "That looks like the beginning of a ravine. And that's where we'll start."

And at that moment he began hearing an animal screaming somewhere up the ravine.

"That sounds like the cry of a jungle cat, Captain."

"Whatever it is, it doesn't sound good to me." Edge hesitated for a moment, then made a decision. "Lieutenant, take Ringo Smith and scout in the direction of those screams."

"Aye, aye, sir!"

Jaleel's eyes lit up at the thought of action. She whirled and ran back toward the ship, calling to Ringo as she passed him, "All right, Smith, we're going on a recon. Get your equipment."

Ringo Smith stared blankly at the lieutenant.

Captain Edge watched from where he stood a few yards out from the cruiser. He well knew that Ringo Smith was not a very combative young man. There was a gentleness in him that Tara Jaleel had never been able to eradicate, no matter how hard she tried. More than anything else, he seemed to want love and approval. He was not likely to get either from Lieutenant Jaleel, Edge reflected.

Reluctantly, Ringo retrieved his weapon, a Neuromag pistol, and then slouched toward him. "Captain, there must be someone better qualified than I am to go out on this kind of a job."

Captain Edge looked down at the Space Ranger. Ringo had mild hazel eyes and was smaller than average for his age. Edge actually had a liking for the boy, although he tried not to show favoritism on board the *Daystar.* The captain thought, *I don't think he'd have much of a chance with a Lo'custra.* However, he knew he could not say such a thing to one of his crew. He had to inspire confidence wherever possible.

Stepping up to meet the Ranger, he did an unusual thing. He put a hand on Ringo's shoulder and said quietly, "Ringo, I know this is a tough job. But it's the hard things that are good for us, not the easy things." He smiled and for a moment lost the appearance of being the hard-driving captain of a star cruiser. He wanted to make a friend of this boy, and he added, "I know it's hard. But you'll be a man soon, and it's things like this that get you ready for being a man. You understand that, Ringo?"

"Yes sir. I guess so." Ringo shifted his feet uncomfortably and then exclaimed almost in despair, "I'll never satisfy Lieutenant Jaleel, though. She thinks I'm nothing but a sissy."

Captain Edge grinned. "Ringo, Lieutenant Jaleel probably thinks the same thing about me." He squeezed the boy's shoulder and said encouragingly, "Now, go on and do a good job." A thought came to him, and he let his hand remain in place a moment longer. "You might impress Ranger St. Clair if you do a good job out there today."

Ringo looked up quickly and felt his face burning. He had not known that Captain Edge was aware of his admiration of Raina. He found himself unable to say a word.

At that moment Lieutenant Jaleel returned and snapped, "Come along, Smith!"

Ringo gave one look at Captain Edge and saw that there was no way out of this assignment. "Thank you, Captain. I'll do my best." He turned and ran after Jaleel.

Fear began to close in upon him, though, as it always did at times like this. He had learned to cover it up somewhat, but as the lieutenant plunged ahead into the evening dimness, strange and awful images of what a Lo'custra might be like came to him. He had no idea of what the creatures looked like up close, but he knew that seeing one would not be a pleasant experience. It never was on these alien planets.

He hurried to keep up with the long strides of Lieutenant Jaleel, and he found himself praying, *God, You'll have to take care of me, because I can't take care of myself.*

Prayer was a comfort to him, and he realized that he was growing a little as a Christian. There was a time when he would not have been able to plunge into danger like this. He was still aware that fear was gnawing at him, but somehow his prayer had given him new strength. As he plunged into the evening dark, he whispered, "Thank You, God," and then he ran as hard as he could to catch up with Jaleel.

"Ericson and Bando, report to the bridge!"

Captain Edge was waiting for them, his face set. He was feeling the pressure of the situation.

"I have a job for you two."

"Yes sir. What is it, sir?" Jerusha asked.

"I want you to make your way to the top of Mount Wildersarn. It may be a hard job. We don't know what's out there. We don't know if there are pathways or anything else. The only thing we're sure of, it's not going to be safe."

"Yes sir, we can do it," Dai said quickly.

"When you get to the peak, I want you to make long-range scans of the desert."

"Yes sir. Anything else?" Jerusha inquired.

"Yes, I want you to scan a Lo'custra—if you can get close to one."

Dai suddenly said, "Captain, perhaps I ought to make this recon alone."

Instantly Jerusha flushed. She faced Dai Bando squarely. "What do you mean 'alone'? The captain wants both of us to go!"

"Jerusha, this is going to be a pretty dangerous thing—"

"Are you saying that I'm not able to take care of myself?" she demanded.

The captain watched the confrontation. Jerusha was a very competitive girl, and she had a fierce temper when aroused. At that moment, it seemed to have been completely stirred up. She planted her feet and thrust her chin out at Dai Bando, having to look up only an inch or two.

"I can take care of myself, Mr. Bando! I may even wind up having to take care of you! Just because you're stronger than most, and faster, doesn't give you a right to think you can do anything! Why, I don't even think you'd even understand how to take the scans!"

Dai looked embarrassed.

She had spoken the exact truth, Edge knew. Dai was not good with electronic equipment.

"I–I guess you're right about that, Jerusha. I'm sorry. I was just thinking of you."

Jerusha's anger appeared to evaporate as quickly as it had been aroused. "Oh, that's all right, Dai. I appreciate your wanting to look out for me, but—"

Edge stopped the exchange. "There's no argument about it— you're both going!" And his voice was definite.

As a matter of fact, Jerusha had put her finger exactly on the reason he had chosen the two of them. Jerusha was capable of doing the scientific work, but it was Dai Bando who had the strength and the speed and the courage to protect her in case they ran into trouble. *They make a good combination,* he thought, *and it's the best I can think of at the moment.*

Aloud the captain said, "You've got to learn to work together, you two. That's the way it is on a crew. We all have some weaknesses—and where we're weak, we have to lean on someone else's strength."

Abruptly Jerusha turned to him and asked, "And what are your weaknesses, Captain Edge?"

It was an impudent and unheard-of question for a crew member to make of a captain, even on a ship where discipline was as relaxed as it was on *Daystar*. Jerusha's face flamed, and she said quickly, "I'm sorry, sir. That was out of line. I didn't mean to ask that. I'm sorry."

A sharp reply had been on Edge's tongue, but when he saw her embarrassment—she appeared to be truly sorry, for once in her life—he smiled. "I expect you know quite a few of my weaknesses already, Ranger. I'm not going to reveal any more of them to you at the present time." Then he put aside his light tone and barked, "All right, get to it! I need that information!"

"Aye, aye, sir!" Both Rangers snapped to attention, then turned and left the bridge.

And as always when he sent these young people out on a mission, Captain Edge was worried. "I just hope nothing happens to them. If I were a praying man, I'd say a prayer," he muttered. He hesitated a moment, then said, "Well, I'll say one anyhow. God, take care of them. I know I don't have any right to ask, but they're both Your servants, so I'm asking You to take a special interest in this mission and don't let them come to grief!"

Mei-Lani and Raina were putting on their combat gear down in Engineering.

"You know, this body armor just slows me down!" Mei-Lani said crossly.

Raina smiled at her friend. "I, for one, am glad we have it. Some of us would already be dead if not for these armor suits. Besides, they're really very light—and very tough. If one of those Lo'custra try to bite us, we'll need these suits. Even if they do slow us down a little."

Mei-Lani looked at herself in the full-length mirror that hung on the door. She placed the helmet on her head and sighed. "Well, it wouldn't hurt for them to look a little more fashionable. I'm going to complain to Commandant Lee the next time I see her."

At that moment Contessa charged into the room. With one leap, she knocked Mei-Lani to the floor.

"How do you feel about the body armor now?" Raina asked. "Any bruises?"

Mei-Lani yelled at Contessa. "Get out of here, dog! You're like a bull in a china shop."

The big black German shepherd licked her helmet visor and trotted out of the room.

"What's a bull in a china shop?" Raina asked curiously.

Mei-Lani got up and headed toward the door. "Never mind!" She was reaching for the doorknob when she glanced back at Raina. She was shocked to see tears in the girl's eyes. Quickly she went back and put a hand on the girl's arm. "Why, Raina, what's wrong?"

"It's just me," Raina said. She dashed her tears away rather fiercely. "I'm such a fool!"

"Don't say that. It's not true!"

"It *is* true!"

"I don't know why you would say such a thing." Mei-Lani was truly puzzled. She put her arm around the older girl. "Can you tell me about it?"

Perhaps, Mei-Lani thought, Raina wanted to talk to someone because they were going out on what could be a dangerous mission. Perhaps she wanted to unburden herself.

"I'm sorry for not listening to you, Mei-Lani."

"Listening to me about what?"

"Oh, about Dai! And how he feels about me! It was just like you said. He's not really interested in me—I mean, not as a *girl.*" She went on to tell Mei-Lani what had happened between her and Dai on their so-called date. "You were right, and I was wrong," she finished angrily. But then she managed a smile and said, "From now on, I'm going to ask your advice where Dai Bando's concerned."

Mei-Lani gave the older girl a hug. "I'll help you the best way I can. But I'm only thirteen . . ."

"But you always know the right thing to say, Mei-Lani. How do you do that?"

"All I can tell you is that God gave me a little common sense. But more than that—I do always try to depend on the Holy Spirit."

"Common sense—*and* the Holy Spirit." Raina stood looking down at the floor for a moment. Then said, "That makes sense. I think that's the best combination there is, Mei-Lani. I'll remember that."

Mei-Lani took Raina's hand then. "We're going into danger. Let's pray right now—for our safety and for all of us who'll be out there."

The two girls bowed their heads and prayed, asking for God's guidance and protective care. When Mei-Lani ended her prayer, saying, "In the name of Jesus, I ask it," she smiled warmly at Raina. Then they walked together out of the engineering sector. "So come on. God's with us," she said. "Who can be against us?"

9

The Only Way Out

Suzerain Brutarius laid his head down on the desk in front of him. Weariness washed over him. Outside, he could hear the shrill cries of battle and the continuous hissing of the Lo'custra as they kept on charging his army's positions. For all his courage, the terrible strain of battle against the frightful invaders had sapped his physical strength. Now, gritting his teeth, he murmured, "I don't see how we can ever survive."

Death had become a daily visitor at the High Castle. The Lo'custra had indeed swarmed upon them like locusts. The creatures seemed to have no fear of death whatsoever. Hundreds of them would allow themselves to be slain to make a ramp by which their fellows could crawl up the walls to attack the castle.

The battle had gone on unceasingly because night and day apparently meant nothing to the Lo'custra. Once they started an attack, they never ceased until they accomplished their objectives.

The sound of an urgent knock brought Brutarius upright, and he wiped indecision and discouragement from his face with a weary hand. "Come in," he called hoarsely.

The door opened, and Commander Harvan entered. He was limping badly, for he had taken a serious wound in his right leg. A bloodstained white rag was tied around his forehead. "Sire," he said, "we cannot hold the castle."

For a moment Brutarius stared in silence at his

chief general. He knew Commander Harvan to be absolutely loyal and as courageous as any Capellan who drew breath. The suzerain said softly, “Is there no hope at all, Commander?”

“We will fight to the last man, but in the end we will be overcome.” Harvan suddenly was weaving as if weakness had overtaken him.

Brutarius rushed to his side. “Here, sit down. You have no business going back to the battle.”

“I must go back. Every man counts, Your Majesty. But again, I must tell you it is a hopeless struggle.”

At that moment Brutarius’s wife entered the room. She took one look at the wounded commander and hurried to bring a basin of water. She began to bathe his face, listening to the two men talk and probably sensing the hopelessness of the situation.

“What is your recommendation then, Commander?” Anmoir asked, straightening up. She took a small bottle from a shelf and poured some of its contents into a glass. “Take some of this,” she said. “It will strengthen you.”

Harvan drank the liquid, and his eyes did brighten at once, but still his brows were drawn down in a scowl. “I wish I had far better news for you both, but there is no hope of holding out. There are too many of them, and they are too powerful. I’ve never seen better armor. Most of our weapons are deflected off it. Our laser cannons have depleted their power reserves. In some cases, we’re fighting the creatures with pistols, swords, and clubs.”

“I had hoped that the rescue fleet from Commandant Lee might have come before now,” Brutarius murmured. He drew back his shoulders then and seemed to shake himself into action. “So again we ask, what must we do, Commander?”

Taking a deep breath, Harvan said quickly and with decision, "You must leave the castle through the tunnel, Your Majesty. I will cover your retreat with the remaining troops."

"You know about the *tunnel?*" Brutarius's eyes were wide with astonishment. "My father told me nobody knew about it but me."

"When your father was suzerain, he felt that he should tell me of its existence in case you were ever hurt and in deadly peril. Sire, you *must* leave the castle. Any minute now, those overgrown insects will come charging through the doors."

"I cannot do that," Brutarius protested. "That would be running away from my people!"

"You must save yourself, Sire. You are the suzerain. You must live to rally the people. Our time will come," he said grimly. "Until then, you must save your life. It is not a matter of courage. No man has ever questioned that."

"I think the commander is right, husband." Anmoir put her hand on his arm and looked up at him earnestly. "It is not a matter at all of your courage. It is the matter of the survival of our people. This is a dark and terrible hour, but the sun will rise again, and you must be there, alive, to lead our people."

For a moment silence reigned in the room, broken only by the sound of battle, the cries of the wounded, and the harsh hissings of the Lo'custra. Brutarius was a stubborn man, and he had longed to be in the fight physically from the beginning. Only the extreme persuasion of his wife and his officers had kept him from the front line.

But suddenly the suzerain sighed heavily. "You may be right, Harvan. But the truth is, we cannot follow Tramere and Sanara."

"Why not, Sire?"

"Because I gave them the only map. We could never find our way through that maze. I remember going through it as just a youngster. There are a thousand turns and a thousand different doorways. We would be lost and die anyway. Better to stay here and die fighting at the wall."

"No, husband, that is *not* what we must do." His wife's eyes were bright as she said, "There is a way that we may be sure that we will not be lost."

"How is that, my dear?"

"Why, it's simple." A smile touched her lips despite the seriousness of the moment. "All we have to do is follow Tramere's giant footprints. You have said yourself that the floor of the tunnel is dirt, not stone. And you know what a tremendous footprint he always leaves. We have seen them often enough."

"She is right, Your Majesty!" Harvan got to his feet, saying, "But you must go quickly!" Even as he spoke, the sounds from outside became louder, and there was urgency in his voice as he said, "Go *now*. Quickly. While there is yet time!"

"Very well, but I will not leave you all here. Our remaining troops are but a handful. Gather together as many survivors as you can. Have them fight a rearguard action that will bring them to this room. Then we will all escape down the tunnel together."

"Yes, Your Majesty. That would be wise. At least that will give you a personal bodyguard." Harvan turned and hurried from the room, and they soon heard his voice shouting orders.

"We are ready, Your Majesty." Harvan was back with the first of the retreating rearguard.

"Come, then. Have the men turn on their torches."

Brutarius opened the secret door and plunged into the tunnel, holding his wife's hand. Then he looked back to see that Harvan was leading the retreat.

"Harvan, are they close?"

"Yes, Your Majesty, and we cannot hold them long. Will you not arrange to close the door?"

"Send the men on ahead with my wife. You and I will remain here."

"Your Majesty, that will solve nothing! You will be killed! Let us shut the door!"

"No, I have a plan. And that is why I will not close the secret door." A smile touched the king's lips as he said, "There's one trick that hasn't been played yet. I have a surprise for these Lo'custra. Now, do as I command you."

The commander was reluctant, but he entrusted Anmoir to the care of General Allo and waited with the suzerain until all of the guard had passed.

The last soldier, a tall, red-headed young man, was panting. He was wounded and had blood on his hands and on his arm, but he drew himself up. "Sire, I will stay and fight to the death."

"You have fought valiantly, my good soldier," Brutarius said kindly, "but now your fate rests on your suzerain. Go and join the others."

Commander Harvan briefly focused his torch on the young soldier as he fled down the passageway and disappeared. Then he turned to the suzerain, saying, "Sire, this is madness. We will both be killed!"

"Come this way, Commander."

"Very well, but I can hear them coming. You hear that hideous hissing they make?"

"Let them hiss. It will not be for long."

Brutarius hurried down the passage. But then, before long, he abruptly stopped. "There it is. Do you see that sign?"

The commander focused his torch upward. Someone had painted a mysterious symbol near the top of the tunnel wall.

"It looks like a kind of cross."

"It is the mark that I remember. It is on the map, but I had forgotten it for a time. Look at this." Brutarius moved to the side of the tunnel, and his hands felt the rock, as though searching. "It must be here somewhere . . ." he murmured. Then he exclaimed with excitement, "*Yes*, here it is!"

There was a clicking, and then a small section of the rock wall rolled back.

"What is that, Your Majesty?"

"You will see what it is. Keep your eye fixed for the enemy. As soon as the first of them appear, tell me."

Commander Harvan stepped back and peered down the way they had come. "They're not far," he murmured. "I hear them." He waited, and the sounds grew louder. Then the screeches and cries and hissings of the Lo'custra filled the tunnel, and Harvan yelled, "There they are, Your Majesty!"

"Good. Let's see if they can combat *this* enemy!" Reaching into the opening in the rock wall, Brutarius seized a lever. With all his strength he pulled it, and as he did so, an ominous groaning seemed to shake the entire mountain.

"What is it, Your Majesty? What have you done?" Harvan cried.

Brutarius did not answer. Indeed, he could not answer—or if he had, his reply would not have been heard. Both men stared as the Lo'custra charged toward them, letting out cries of victory.

But even as they came on, the mountain shook, and suddenly from over the Lo'custra the roof simply caved in. Now the roar of falling rock and the dust from the closing of the tunnel filled the air. Both men stood listening as the howls of the enemy ceased. And when the rocks had finally settled, they saw that the tunnel was closed forever.

"We'll never be able to use this escape route again."

"No, Sire, but it saved us now."

"Come," said the suzerain. "We must join the others. There is still hope, my friend!"

Sitting before the communication panels on the *Daystar*, Raina and Mei-Lani worked desperately. They were tired. They had sat for hours with their eyes fixed on the dials and screen displays, hoping to pick up the Lo'custran signals. At the same time, both of them were praying for Jaleel and Ringo, for Jerusha and Dai.

When Raina was about to give up hope of their hearing anything, Mei-Lani said, "Look—what's this, Raina?" She turned up the volume, and undoubtedly there was a pattern of clicks sounding just under the hissing noises.

"These clicks are being produced at a sound range that our ears can't normally hear," Mei-Lani said. "Thank goodness we have this equipment. I hate to say it, but Heck knows his stuff!"

"I think the clicks are getting closer together now!" Raina exclaimed. She listened with all her might to the patterns, and then suddenly a thought came to her. Turning to Mei-Lani, she said, "I think the Lo'custra must have seen the *Daystar* land. It sounds to me as if the clicking pattern shows them closing in on *this* sector."

The girls struggled to sort out the signals.

Finally Mei-Lani said, "We've got to do something!" She touched the signal device on her belt and cried out, "Hector Jordan, come to Communications!"

"What do you want Heck for?" Raina asked. She liked Heck but had little confidence in anything except his ability with computers.

Mei-Lani said, "I think he may have something that we're going to have to use." But she said no more just then.

In minutes, Heck rushed in, burdened down with a mass of equipment. "I've got all my stuff here," he said, grinning broadly. "I knew you'd be calling on old Heck to save the day." He began to lay out his gear.

"What *are* those things?" Raina asked as he put down one strange-looking device after another.

"Why, my dear Raina, these tools were designed by little ol' humble me! Tell me you're not impressed."

"I'll be impressed if they work. And you are a light-year away from being either little or humble!" Raina turned her attention back to the computer console.

As Heck worked with his equipment and Mei-Lani urged him on, Raina was silent. She kept thinking of Dai Bando primarily. She knew that, if there was danger, he would be right in the middle of it. She had noticed that he seemed to have no sense at all of personal safety but would throw himself into any situation if he thought it would help someone else.

"Hurry up, Heck!" Mei-Lani begged.

"Well, I'm working as fast as I can, aren't I?"

At that moment Contessa came padding into Communications. She was carrying a piece of Heck's equipment in her mouth—something he must have dropped in the corridor without noticing. The intelligent animal knew by the smell that it was Heck's and had brought it to him. She padded over to his chair and put one forepaw on his shoulder.

"Hey, what are you doing?" Heck yelled, turning around and seeing the monstrous animal.

"She brought something to you, Heck. Did you lose it?"

At Raina's question, Heck suddenly peered at the item in the dog's mouth.

"Well, I'll be dipped!" he exclaimed. "It's a good thing you found this, girl. I wouldn't get anywhere without it." He reached for the device. And when Contessa put the piece of equipment in his hand, she suddenly licked his face.

"Hey, no kissing now! I haven't got time for it!" But Heck grinned. He shoved his hand in his pocket and brought out one of his favorite candy bars. "I wouldn't give this to anybody but you, Contessa, but today you earned it." He stripped off the paper and extended the chocolate to the dog. He watched her eat it, and then he sighed. "That was the last one of those I had. I hope you appreciate it."

The German shepherd swallowed the last morsel, reared up, and licked his face again.

"Get away, now! You females can't get enough of me, can you?" Heck winked at Raina and said, "You'll have your turn later, Raina, as soon as I save us all from this mess you've gotten us into." He turned back to the board, and his hands began racing over the switches as Raina and Mei-Lani looked on with apprehension.

10

Chosen to Lead

"Hurry *up*, Ringo. We've got to get back!"

Ringo was so immersed in his task that for a moment he had forgotten to be afraid. The scanning device that he held was highly sensitive and was running several different types of scans at the same time. Its accurate operation depended on Ringo's complete concentration. Otherwise, the data would be useless.

Glancing at Tara Jaleel, he said, "I just have to make a few more scans, Lieutenant."

Lieutenant Jaleel shrugged impatiently.

Tara Jaleel knew better than the boy the danger that lay all around them. It was as though she had a sixth sense about danger. It was an element to her—like air or water. She could smell it, or taste it, or feel it on the surface of her skin. Now she sensed that danger was all around, and although she had no fear for herself, she was responsible for getting herself and Ringo back to the ship safely. "How many more readings do you have to take?"

"Just a few. I know that Mei-Lani and Raina will need these scans in order to do their job."

Jaleel stared at him, then said, "It could cost us our lives, you know."

Instantly Ringo looked up, and suddenly he was aware of the tension in the lieutenant's body. He saw that her face was tense, and he thought, *If Jaleel is a little bit apprehensive, that's the same thing as somebody else screaming with fear.* Now he glanced around nervously, bit his lip, but then shook his head. "I've got to get them. I'll hurry."

"All right, but do it as fast as you can."

Ringo worked furiously, moving from spot to spot. At one point he became aware of some faint noises. "Is that the Lo'custra?" he whispered.

"It's not mice."

Ringo blinked at the abrupt answer and swallowed hard. "All right," he said. "Just one more." He took the scan, then grabbed up his equipment and scrambled to where the lieutenant was standing, peering out at something he could not see. "I'm ready," he gasped.

"Then follow me—and don't fall behind!"

As they wound their way back to the *Daystar*, Ringo was more and more conscious of the tension in the lieutenant. He was also conscious that the noises he had been hearing were becoming louder. He ran hard, but still his short legs could not keep up with those of Lieutenant Jaleel. Now and then she had to wait for him.

As he ran, Ringo tried to keep his eyes fixed on what was straight ahead. He suddenly remembered something that Mei-Lani Lao had once told him. She said there was an athlete back on Earth years ago—a black baseball player—who said a lot of rather wise things in a funny way. One saying was that, if you hear footsteps, don't look back—something might be gaining on you!

Ringo felt he knew exactly what that meant, for something *was* behind him. And gaining on him. He gasped, "Something wicked this way comes, Lieutenant!"

Jaleel said, "Then run faster!"

Panting for breath, Ringo Smith exerted every

ounce of his strength as he and Tara Jaleel raced back toward the *Daystar.*

Tramere and the princess burst into the clearing at the top of the mountain.

"The hut—there's the hut!" Tramere panted. The big man leaned against a small tree that gave with his weight. He drew his breath in great gasps. "We made it here safely, Princess! We made it!"

Sanara seemed not as exhausted as her protector. Of course, she had far less weight to carry. She took a few hesitant steps toward the hut and said, "Is this the right place, Tramere?"

"It's the only one," he panted. He studied the structure. "Yes, I remember it. I was one of those who brought supplies here at your father's command. The hut is just as it was the last time I was here."

The small cabin was utilitarian in appearance and had no frills in its architecture. Large brown logs, stacked one atop the other, formed the walls. The roof appeared oversized, for it appeared the building had been made waterproof with pitch and gravel. The gravel was identical in color to the stones that littered the ground. Large boulders were strewn around the hut like giant marbles. The shelter would be virtually invisible from the air, Tramere thought. Its builder had made the hut for survival in the mountain elements, but having only one door made it impractical for fighting.

The sun was down now. Only a thin crimson line showed along the horizon. But still, in its faint last light, as they looked down from their lofty peak, they could see for miles across the desert below.

"The Lo'custra," Sanara said. "They're everywhere!"

"Yes, I didn't know there were so many of them."

"And look, Tramere. Some are climbing up Mount Wildersarn toward us!"

Tramere did not answer. He had limitless courage, but he knew that for a lone man and a girl facing the battle hordes of the Lo'custra, there was simply no hope. He looked downward to where the invaders had begun to swarm up the side of the mountain.

He had seen them by the castle. It was hard to imagine a worse nightmare. Now he could imagine their green-and-brown bodies jumping from rock to rock as nimble as any mountain goat. Their heads were gruesome. Their hissing noises caused one to freeze in his tracks with fear. Tramere estimated that the Lo'custra would be at their shelter in less than two hours.

"We must eat," Tramere said, and the two went inside the hut. The big man knew that danger was coming and had no idea of how they might escape it, but he did know that they needed strength.

"Let me see what supplies are here," Sanara said. "And then I'll fix us a meal. I can do that."

"All right. Women can always cook better than men, I suppose."

"My mother taught me how." She examined the metal canisters and burlap bags. "Now it's all starting to make sense," she commented as she took long strips of dried, dark meat from one of the storage tins.

"What do you mean—'make sense'? Nothing about this makes sense to me!" the giant bellowed as he examined the edge of his sword.

Sanara laughed and then said, "I don't mean those insects out there. I mean that my mother taught me to cook this kind of food. It's terrible-tasting if you compare it with the usual food we eat at the castle. But every month or two, Mother would go into the kitchen and cook *this* stuff herself." She reached into a burlap bag and pulled out a handful of dried vegetables. "Then we'd have it for supper. It was like a ritual to my parents."

"A ritual?"

"Exactly. They told me that eating this poor food reminded them of our heritage—the roots of our family thousands of years ago."

"Your parents are noble people, Sanara. What's good enough for them is certainly good enough for us. Who knows? Capellans might have to start all over again if this planet survives and any of us are left alive."

"I have a feeling we'll survive—somehow," Sanara said as she tore the dried meat into bite-sized chunks.

They ate ravenously, for they had not had anything for hours, and then they both went outside. It was completely dark now, and they could not see down the mountain, but Tramere sensed the approach of the Lo'custra.

"I think they'll wait till dawn," he said. "And maybe by that time the cruisers will get here from Intergalactic Command."

"Do you really think so, Tramere?"

"I always try to think good things."

Actually, Tramere did not have much hope, but he did not want to discourage the girl. The big man peered down into her face as she sat beside him, and suddenly he put a protective arm around her.

That seemed to give Sanara a sense of security, and she whispered, "I'm glad you're here with me, Tramere."

They sat in silence for a time, and then Tramere spoke. There was an unusually serious tone to his voice. "Princess, I have something to say to you."

"Yes, what is it?"

"We don't know how much time we have. The Lo'custra may wait till dawn, but they may be coming now, even in the darkness. The only thing I'm sure of is that they will come."

"What is it you want to tell me, Tramere?"

"I want to tell you a story from the Bible."

"That's the book you read so much—the book that tells about your God."

"Yes, it is. Now, please listen carefully, Princess. Once there was a kingdom much like ours, and God was very concerned about His people. They had had a very bad king for some time, and now there was going to be a new king, but nobody knew that but God Himself."

"Your God knows everything, doesn't He, Tramere?"

"Yes, He knows the past, He knows the present, and He knows the future."

"How strange," Sanara murmured, "to know the future."

"I cannot understand it, but that is what my Bible tells me. Now listen carefully, little one. There was a young man out in the wilder parts of the country. He was about your age, I would guess."

"What was his name?"

"His name was David. He was the youngest son of the house, and his father had put him to keeping the sheep."

"Was he a good shepherd?"

"The very finest." Tramere smiled. "He was very brave too, for when a lion would come, or a wolf, or a bear, David would take his sling, put a stone in it, and he was so good with that sling that he could kill the animal with one stone."

"Did they not have laser cannons?"

"Nothing but spears, and knives, and swords. And David had a sling."

Tramere's story went on for some time. He wanted to keep the girl's mind occupied with something other than what was coming, and he went into great detail telling about the boyhood of David. Finally he said, "One day a prophet came to David's house—"

"What's a prophet?"

"A prophet was a man or a woman sent by God to tell the people something they needed to know."

"I wish we had prophets," Sanara said wistfully. "I'd like to know what God says. I'd like to know the future."

"Sometimes it's better not to. But in any case, the prophet came. Now, David had many brothers, all of them taller and stronger than he. The prophet said to David's father, 'One of your sons will be the next king.'"

"I'll bet his father was happy about that. I'll bet he was happy for David."

"No, he didn't know yet what God wanted. He brought out his firstborn son, a big, tall, strong fellow, and the prophet thought, *Surely this must be the new king. He's so big and strong and noble-looking.* But God said to him, 'No, this is not the one I have chosen to lead My people.'

"He didn't choose the oldest, and He didn't choose the second oldest, either, although I suppose he was almost as large and as strong," Tramere said. "One by one, David's father brought in all his boys, but each time God said to the prophet, 'This is not the one.' Finally the prophet said, 'Do you have any more sons?'

"'Yes,' David's father said, 'I have one younger son, but he is just a boy. He's out taking care of the sheep.'

"'Bring him to me,' the prophet commanded.

"It took some time, but finally David was brought

in from the field. He was a fine-looking young chap with rosy cheeks. He had been outdoors all of his life, and he was so handsome that I think your heart would have thrilled to have seen him, Princess."

"What happened, Tramere?"

"'Well, as soon as the prophet saw David, he took out a little bottle of oil and poured some on David's head—he anointed David king over all the people."

"Why would he do that? What does anointed mean?"

"That is when someone poured oil over another to show God's approval. You see, God had approved David to be king."

"Was he a good king?"

"The best king that any kingdom ever had. He was the only man of whom it was said that he was a man after God's own heart!"

Sanara looked into his face. "Why are you telling me this story, Tramere?"

"I'm telling you this because I believe God has anointed you to lead your people."

Sanara looked stunned. "Why, Tramere, are you a prophet?"

"Not at all. As one man in the Bible said, I am neither a prophet nor the son of a prophet." He smiled gently. "No, Princess, I'm not a prophet, but there is no prophet here, so I believe God spoke to my heart. And He has assured me that you will indeed be the leader of your people someday."

Suddenly Tramere drew a small bottle from somewhere inside his garments. "This is a bottle of fine oil. I have been saving it ever since God spoke to me. Now," he said, "I anoint you as leader of *your* people." He poured a little oil into his hand, and then with his huge fingers touched her forehead with it. "The God of the heavenly host has chosen you."

"Your God?" she whispered.

"There is only one God. He is the God that I have told you of—the God of the Bible."

As she sat beside the giant, the oil still on her forehead, Sanara said simply, "I think I would like to serve your God, Tramere. Always."

A great joy came to the giant, and he could not speak for a moment. Then tears ran down his face. "If worse comes to worst, remember, Princess, He is the God of deliverance. He delivered David from the mouth of the lion and from the paw of the bear, and—whatever happens—He is able to deliver you from any danger!"

And then Tramere told the princess about Jesus.

11
The Girl in the Dream

Captain Mark Edge had been watching from one of the *Daystar*'s portholes. Suddenly he straightened up. "There!" he said, his voice colored with relief. "There come Lieutenant Jaleel and Ringo."

Temple Cole, who had been standing beside him, edged in closer. The porthole was small, and he did not move a great deal. "What good news that is!" she said.

Captain Edge was suddenly conscious of her closeness. Without thinking, he put an arm around her.

"You're hugging me," she said but did not pull away.

"Am I?"

"Of course, you are. Don't pretend you don't know it!"

"I'm not always aware of what I do when I am under pressure." Edge smiled down at her. "Sometimes it takes me ten or fifteen minutes before I can come to myself."

The ship's surgeon laughed. "You never give up, do you, Mark?"

Just that minute Studs Cagney rushed in, his face filled with excitement. "Captain," he yelled, "Jaleel and Smith are coming back! Do you see them?"

Captain Edge spun around. "Of course, I see them! Do you think I'm blind?"

Cagney blinked with surprise at the harsh words, then must have suddenly realized that he had interrupted something. "Sorry," he mumbled and backed away. "I just thought you'd want to know that they're coming back safe."

"You shouldn't have yelled at him like that, Mark," Temple said gently, when Studs was gone.

The captain ran a hand through his blond hair. "I know. It's just that—well, I guess I've been pretty uptight about our recon people. And I'm *still* worried about Dai and Jerusha."

"Maybe they'll be back soon, if Jaleel and Smith are here."

Captain Edge and the doctor headed for the bridge, where Raina St. Clair and Mei-Lani Lao soon joined them. The girls were excited. They had just become aware that Jaleel and Ringo had been sighted coming back.

Accompanying them was Heck. He swaggered in front of Captain Edge and said loudly, "Well, Captain, I guess you can relax."

"What do you mean by that, Jordan?"

"I mean I've broken the Lo'custra language."

"*You* broke the language!" Raina exploded. "It was Mei-Lani who did most of it!"

"She couldn't have done it without my help. It was all a matter of finding the key, and I did it with my lovely creations." He had brought along one of his instruments and now launched into a description of how he had rushed to the help of the two girls.

"They did their best, but what can you expect from a couple of girls, Captain? You and I are men of the world, aren't we?"

"Men of the world!" Tara Jaleel appeared at the entrance to the bridge, and her face was dark with anger. "I'll tell you what I'd like to do, Captain!" she snarled. "I'd like to tie up this nincompoop and use him as bait for the Lo'custra!"

The very thought of such a thing seemed enough to silence Heck Jordan. Everyone knew he was dreadfully afraid of Tara Jaleel anyway. He contented himself by muttering, "That's the thanks I get for saving everyone!"

"How does it work, Heck—this device of yours?" the captain asked.

"First of all, it's the matter of the right frequency range," Heck explained, less boastfully now. "After I determined that, I had to isolate the source of the clicking noises." He turned the crescent-shaped device in his hand. "When I determined that the clicking noises are made by their head spines, all I had to do was interpolate the type of hissing that mixed with the clicks."

"And that's how you translated their language?" Captain Edge responded.

Raina interrupted. "That's when *Mei-Lani* translated the language!"

The captain turned to Mei-Lani. "And . . ."

Mei-Lani took over. "It's true that without Heck's gizmos we could not have registered the patterns of the clicks and hisses. But, Captain, these are not *intelligent* beings. They are just what they appear to be—giant, very ferocious insects. One pattern means 'I found food.' Another pattern means 'Attack.' Still another pattern means 'Search,' and so on. There aren't any patterns of communication that indicate anything more than a rudimentary insect-type intelligence. Imagine a flea being ten feet tall. It would be big, but it would still be a flea!"

The captain grabbed the arms of his chair. "So what you're telling me is that Capella is being destroyed by a bunch of *insects?*"

Mei-Lani spoke in a low voice. "Actually, a form of a space locust, Captain. The name Lo'custra loosely translates 'the devourers who conquer.'"

Heck was fidgeting and couldn't wait to interrupt. "So you see, being one of the men of the world that we are, I was able to combine the signal imputes from the Lo'custra through the short-range scanners and medical audio surgical extractor. After that, I processed all the data through the Communications computer language banks." Heck grinned a toothy grin. "Nobody would have thought to do that but me!"

By the time Heck had finished his explanation, he seemed to have temporarily lost his fear of Tara Jaleel.

"You think there'll be a bonus in it for me for finding this?" he asked Captain Edge.

"I'll be sure to take it up with Commandant Lee, Jordan."

Edge's voice was ironic, but Heck was not usually able to discern anything such as this. He grinned broadly and winked at Mei-Lani. "You see, babe. You stick with me, and I'll teach you a few things."

Captain Edge left the bridge then and went to his private quarters. There he sat down before the screen on his computer console.

"This is a priority level nine communication to Commandant Winona Lee."

"DNA retina scan. Place finger in receptacle," the computer said.

Edge placed his finger into the identification slot while a red beam from the computer scanned his retina.

"Identification verified. Captain Mark Edge, commanding *Daystar*."

Soon the image of Commandant Lee was flickering in front of him.

"Commandant Lee, I have a serious report."

"Let's have your report, Captain."

Edge then told the commandant all that they had found out about the Lo'custra. "The situation here is critical. It's worse than you thought. The planet is doomed unless we get help at once."

"The fleet is on its way even now, Captain Edge. Can you hold out, or do you need to leave at once?"

"I *can't* leave. Two of my crew members are still out on a recon, and I fear that the Lo'custra are headed this way."

"Hold out as long as you can, Captain. But you know how it is. Every crew member knew that he might lose his life in the service. You'll have to leave them behind to save the rest of the crew, if necessary."

"I don't like the sound of that, Commandant."

"I don't care whether you like it or not, Captain!" Commandant Lee snapped crisply. "I would give the same orders if *you* were outside the ship and the situation was the same. Do you understand me now?"

"Yes, Commandant, I understand perfectly," Edge said grimly. "But I must protest, and I'll tell you flat that I don't like it."

"I don't like it either, Captain Edge, but we weren't put in positions of command to do the things we like! We were put here to do our duty, and that's what I expect you to do!"

The Lo'custra were very close now. Sanara expected to see them come over the rise at any second. Their hissing was almost overwhelming her senses.

"Princess, I want you to stay by the door of the hut. If you have to, lock yourself in."

New fear gripped Sanara, but she said, "Tramere, I'm not going in there and let you fight by yourself."

"You must! I will go to the other side of the clearing now and try to draw them toward me. With God's help, maybe I can distract them and they won't discover you."

As Sanara stood watching, the giant ran to a place perhaps sixty yards away from the hut, where he began waving his long sword back and forth and yelling in a thunderous voice.

And then several Lo'custra came over the hill. They spotted Tramere immediately and rushed toward him.

The giant struck fast and hard. His sword flashed like lightning as he stabbed the creatures in the one spot he had told Sanara was vulnerable—a spot just behind their front legs. Since they were without armor plating on this part of their bodies, when a sword struck home, the insect was killed instantly.

But for every Lo'custra he slew, two more seemed to take its place. And now not only were the insects attacking Tramere, but they were also devouring their slain comrades. Sanara was astonished at their brutality.

Tramere appeared to be growing tired, and Sanara could do nothing to help her friend. She would not even be able to lift his sword with her small strength.

But suddenly a thought came to her: *Sanara, pray to the God of the Bible.*

The golden-haired princess bowed her head and began to pray.

"Jerusha, hurry. We must get to the top," Dai urged.

"I'm coming! I'm right behind you."

As they topped the hill, the first thing Jerusha saw was a huge man slashing and stabbing with his sword at a swarm of attacking Lo'custra.

Dai looked back at her. "Aim your Neuromag at the soft spot just behind their front legs! They've no armor there."

Firing his own Neuromag, Dai advanced toward

the attacking insects and pressed in close to help the big man.

Jerusha came up behind him, but stayed on the fringe of the battle, shooting at the creatures from there just as fast as she could press the trigger.

"There's too many of them!" she screamed.

And then she saw that Dai was completely surrounded by Lo'custra. They were closing in, trying to thrust him through with their head spines, but he was too quick for them. He somersaulted out of their midst, firing his Neuromag at their vulnerable spots at the same time.

"I've got to help the giant!" he yelled to Jerusha. "You get back to *Daystar* and tell the captain to be prepared for anything."

"You'll be killed!" she shouted between Neuromag volleys. Her voice was tight with fear, and her body was responding out of pure reflex. "You don't stand a chance!"

"Go! I'm depending on you. I'll get the giant out of this, and we'll be following you within minutes."

Jerusha turned and sped away. Had she seen Dai Bando for the last time?

Dai saw that the insects had backed the big man into a hollow in the mountainside. He was hemmed in by the horrible creatures. He lifted his sword for a blow to the nearest Lo'custra, but the insect lowered its head and lunged at him. The last cry out of the giant's mouth was the name of Jesus.

Dai Bando watched it all with horror. He knew that in seconds the insects would began devouring the body, and he turned sadly away from the scene. He would follow Jerusha back to the *Daystar*.

And then he spotted something out of the corner

of his eye. It was a small cabin on the far side of the clearing. He looked closer. A girl was on her knees just in front of the door!

He raced toward her.

As he drew near, she looked up at him with tears running down her cheeks. "Are you an angel?" she asked sincerely. "I've been praying."

And when Dai saw her face, he knew it was the girl he had seen in his dream. The girl whose smile had so touched him. The girl with the golden hair.

"No, I'm not an angel." He smiled. "My name is Dai Bando. And you keep praying—we're not out of danger yet." He reached down his hand to her. "Don't be afraid. I need to put you over my shoulder. I'll carry you away from here."

Dai picked her up and threw her across his shoulder as if she weighed nothing. A glance across the clearing told him that the Lo'custra were beginning to look about for further victims. He flung himself over the rise and down to the next rock ledge. Then he ran like the wind.

I just hope Jerusha gets to Daystar *and briefs Captain Edge,* he thought. *Because I'm bringing the enemy straight back to the ship!*

He could hear the hissing of the Lo'custra as they pursued him.

12
A Matter of Seconds

Tension had reached almost an intolerable level on board the *Daystar.* According to all the instrument readings, the Lo'custra were closing in on every side.

"I can't tell how many there are, Captain, but there are too many for us," Zeno Thrax said quietly. He had come up to stand beside the captain on the bridge, and now he was studying Captain Edge's face.

Thrax had learned to know his captain well over several missions, and he could read the signs of inner turmoil quite easily. Edge's face was drawn into a mask as if it were frozen, and his eyelids half covered his blue-gray eyes. If this were not enough, he kept reaching up to touch his right earlobe in a nervous gesture that Thrax had come to recognize. It always revealed that the captain was either worried, or agitated, or angry.

"We'll wait as long as we can, Zeno."

"What were the orders from Commandant Lee, if I may ask?"

"She said that we're to disengage before action."

Thrax thought for a moment, then asked, "Does that mean leaving the Rangers to their fate?"

"That's exactly what it means."

"Did you protest the order, sir?"

"Of course, I protested it! What do you think?"

"No offense, Captain." Thrax shrugged his shoulders. "I know you're very concerned about Ericson and

Bando. It would be a shame if we had to abandon them, but orders are orders."

Edge touched his ear, then shifted his feet and suddenly put his hands behind his back, clenching them. Zeno Thrax knew the captain liked to preserve a stern countenance when under stress. He guessed that Edge realized that his first officer had seen through his little act.

"It's easy enough for Lee to sit out there somewhere and send these young people to their deaths, but I'm responsible for them."

"No more than she is. Commandant Lee ordered the mission."

"But she doesn't have to watch it, as I do." Suddenly Edge stared at Zeno Thrax, who hoped his own face revealed very little. "Don't you ever lose it, Thrax?"

"Lose it? Lose what, sir?"

"Lose your composure! Don't you ever blow up? That face of yours is like a white mask, and I can never tell what's going on inside of you. Do you ever *feel* anything?"

Zeno Thrax did not answer immediately. He was hurt by the captain's words for, despite his rather stern features and colorless eyes, he did feel things, deeply at times. He was very fond of both Jerusha Ericson and Dai Bando, and it hurt him to think that the captain should think he was indifferent to their danger.

"Yes sir, I do feel something."

The short answer of his first officer stopped Edge in his tracks. "Sorry, Zeno," he said. He reached out and touched the other man's shoulder. "I'm not myself, I guess."

The two continued standing on the bridge, watching the digital clock tick off the seconds, both knowing that there was no way to avoid Commandant Lee's orders and both hating the idea of abandoning the two Rangers.

In Navigation, Temple Cole was standing with Navigator Bronwen Llewellen. They were staring out a porthole. As a matter of fact, every porthole on the cruiser was occupied, for the whole ship was aware of the order for liftoff within minutes.

"I can't believe that Captain Edge will abandon Jerusha and Dai," Dr. Cole said. The very idea of leaving the two to certain death sent a chill over her, and she bit her lip nervously.

"Captain Edge would never do such a thing unless he had orders." Bronwen Llewellen's voice was calm, but there was a small tremor in it.

It was unusual for Bronwen to show alarm or concern. Indeed, as far as Temple Cole was concerned, it was the first time she had ever seen agitation of any sort in the navigator. She leaned closer to look into Bronwen's face, but the woman quickly turned her head, making that impossible.

"You're worried, aren't you, Bronwen?"

"He's my only living relative," the navigator said quietly. "I love him dearly. His father was my brother. I was closer to him than anyone else on earth. It would grieve me to be alone, the last person alive of my family."

The enormity of what Bronwen was saying struck Temple, and she took a quick, involuntary breath. Then, without meaning to, she put her arm around the older woman. "I'm sorry, Bronwen," she whispered.

Bronwen Llewellen was not a woman who needed a great deal of comforting. She was strong in spirit, but the idea of losing her nephew and, of course, Jerusha

Ericson as well, was like a burden on her. Long ago she had learned to throw her burdens on the Lord, but somehow this was different.

He's my only kin, she thought again. And despite her strength, the darkness seemed to close in. She peered anxiously toward the foot of the mountain, praying again for the two Rangers who were somewhere on it.

"You believe that God will save them, Bronwen?"

"I'm asking Him to do it."

"But what if He doesn't?"

"I would grieve, but that would not shake my faith in God. Sometimes it's His will for His own to suffer. He sends all of us into the valley from time to time. Sometimes we can't see any farther than a few feet ahead. Sometimes it seems as though all is lost." Bronwen hesitated, and then her voice grew stronger. "But God knows how to run His world, Dr. Cole. He is Lord of the valley, and He is there in every tragedy. If Dai and Jerusha are lost, I will have to say, 'The Lord gave and the Lord has taken away.'"

Even as she spoke these words, a shout came from Heck Jordan. *"There they are!"* Heck had his face pressed against a port twenty feet down the length of the cruiser. "I see them coming—over there by those rocks!"

A cheer went up throughout the *Daystar.*

Captain Edge rushed to a porthole on the Wildersarn side. "It's the Rangers!" he exclaimed. But then he paused and squinted, for he saw that only one figure was coming, not two. And then he said to Zeno Thrax, who had followed him, "There's Jerusha—but no sign of Dai."

"We'd better take her on board, Captain. We don't have much time."

Captain Edge was there to meet Jerusha at the *Daystar* portal. As soon as she stepped into the ship, he pulled her to him and, despite protocol, gave her a hug. "You're all right?" he asked. His voice was not steady.

Jerusha was amazed at the captain's reaction. "I'm all right," she whispered. "I'm fine."

Edge released her as others came rushing up.

It was Bronwen Llewellen who asked, "Where is Dai, Jerusha?"

"He said—he said he'd be coming right behind me! There was a man—and some Lo'custra—and—" She turned and looked back wildly. "I don't know where he is!"

"Captain, only four minutes to liftoff," Zeno Thrax broke in.

"Get to your stations!" Captain Edge commanded.

"But what about Dai?" Jerusha cried. "We can't leave without Dai!"

"Get to your station, Ranger!" Edge ordered. "There's no time to go into Commandant Lee's orders."

She whirled toward the cruiser door, saying, "I won't leave without him! I'll stay and fight with him!"

"You'll go to your position!" The captain caught her arm, then pushed the switch that closed the portal. He looked at the clock. "He's got three minutes. Then the *Daystar* will have to leave. We have no other option."

Bronwen came to Jerusha's side and said softly, "I'm thankful you're safe, Jerusha."

"But Dai—we *can't* go off and leave him!"

"We have three minutes. That's enough." There

was a calmness about the older woman's voice. She bowed her head, and her lips began to move.

When Jerusha had emerged from the foot of the mountain, she was still supposing that Dai was coming behind her. Now she realized that he must have stayed on the mountaintop to hold off the Lo'custra and save her. Staring at the clock embedded in the bulkhead, she watched the second hand sweep around and around. The pointer moved so swiftly that she held her breath, as though trying to slow it by force of will.

"One minute to liftoff!" Zeno Thrax's voice echoed over the intercom.

All over the *Daystar*, officers and men were preparing to leave Capella. Mark Edge's face was white, but his jaw was set. Even Jerusha knew that he really had no choice.

"Thirty seconds to blast off!" Zeno's voice crackled. "Twenty seconds—ten seconds—"

"Look, there he is!" Jerusha screamed the words, for she had seen Dai emerge from the woods.

Dai could feel the Lo'custra practically snapping at his heels. A horde of the insects was about to overtake him and the girl he carried. Once they were on the flat rock of the ledge, the creatures were able to move much quicker.

But then, troops suddenly emerged from a hole in the mountainside to his right. Their leader—Suzerain Brutarius himself, he would learn later—shouted, "Attack!" and the soldiers rushed between Dai and the savage insects, diverting their attention.

At the same time, Zeno Thrax, Tara Jaleel, Ringo Smith, and Jerusha Ericson burst from the *Daystar*, firing their Neuromags as they too ran toward the Lo'custra.

Meantime, other of Brutarius's troops escorted the suzerain's wife to the ship.

Dai ran on toward *Daystar.* He planned to leave Sanara in safety and then return to the battle. But as he wheeled to run back, he saw Brutarius and his soldiers, along with the four *Daystar* crewmen, bolting toward him. Pursuing them were what must have been a thousand of the giant insects.

Jerusha was screaming at the *Daystar*. "Lift off! Lift off!"

And as soon as the last human was aboard, the cruiser's portal closed. Moments later, *Daystar* lifted from the surface of Capella. Many of the Lo'custra leaped after the cruiser with all their might, and in so doing plunged over the rock ledge and fell hundreds of feet to their death.

Then Captain Edge used the ship's thrusters to maneuver *Daystar*'s engines.

"On my mark, fire," he ordered Zeno Thrax.

When the engines pointed directly at the remaining horde of creatures, Captain Edge ordered, "Fire!"

Even Lo'custran armor was no match for the heat of the spaceship's engines. As *Daystar* cleared the mountain, her crew saw that the last of the attacking swarm had been burned to a crisp.

Captain Edge piloted the craft then out over the Great Central Plain.

"Look there, Captain." Bronwen pointed toward the Lo'custra space pods resting on the plain. "It appears they have repaired their pods."

Indeed, they could see thousands of Lo'custra trekking back toward the pods. In some way the insects must have known that the pods would be leaving soon.

"There's not enough power on this whole ship that

would defeat that army," Captain Edge said as he adjusted his flight controls.

Brutarius rubbed his face, then leaned his chin on his hand as he examined the viewer in front of him. His wife, brought safely aboard by General Allo, stood at his side and slid her arm under his. "You did all that you could do," she said earnestly and with much affection in her voice.

"If something doesn't happen soon," Brutarius answered in a solemn voice, "we in this ship will be the lone survivors of Capella."

Sanara rested her hand on her father's strong back. "Father, I've come to believe in the God of Tramere. The only possibility I saw was death, but He made me think to pray, and I did. I never thought at the time that I would be saved by a spaceship. Maybe we should pray some more, Father."

13
Sanara and Dai

The *Daystar* gracefully rose and headed into orbit around Capella.

"Captain Pursey to Captain Edge." The bridge intercom blared surprisingly. It was the captain of Commandant Lee's flagship.

"Edge here. Go ahead, Captain," Edge responded.

"I need you to leave orbit around Capella and take a position by Capella's moon. The fleet will be arriving in moments, and we don't want to shoot down *Daystar* by accident."

"How many ships are coming?" Edge asked.

"Ten in this group with another ten standing by as reinforcements." Pursey was interrupted for a moment, then he continued. "Our plan is to place ten Deep Space Magnum Cruisers around the planet. Our data indicates that only twenty pods are on the ground, and it appears the bulk of the Lo'custra are located near the pods. Pursey out."

Captain Edge positioned *Daystar* near Capella's moon as ordered, just as the first of the rescue cruisers arrived.

The crew watched the battle from the ports. In short order, the overwhelming firepower of the commandant's cruisers destroyed both the pods and the insect invaders clustered near them.

Then troop ships departed from the cruisers, and the air was suddenly filled with flying vessels bent on annihilating any remaining Lo'custra. Guided by

Magnum Cruiser scanners, the troop ships finally eradicated the last of the creatures on the planet. The entire operation took less than a day.

The Lo'custran invaders had been destroyed. But this did not bring back all the human beings and wildlife that the Lo'custra had slain without mercy.

Sanara, of course, had never been on a star cruiser before. Now as she stood looking into the viewer, her eyes were wide with astonishment. She told Dai that she had no idea such terrible power existed.

Dai Bando had helped General Allo get the suzerain and his wife aboard and then saw to the quartering of the remnants of the army that had escaped through the tunnel with them. Now he stood looking down at the princess, who seemed hypnotized by the magnitude of space. He smiled and said, "It's *big*, isn't it, Sanara?"

"I—I had no idea."

She looked up at him, and he saw with shock that there were tears in her eyes.

"Why, what's wrong?" he asked quickly. And he thought that she was one of the most beautiful girls he had ever seen.

"I don't know how to thank you, Dai," she whispered, her voice soft and her lips trembling. "If you hadn't come, we would all have died."

"Well," Dai said, always embarrassed by gratitude, "I didn't exactly do it all myself." He waved toward the screen. "The entire Galactic Command had something to do with your rescue."

"I know. But it was you who came for *me*." Then she smiled brilliantly and lightly touched his chest. "If you hadn't come just when you did, the Lo'custra would have killed me just as they did—"

Seeing that she could not finish what she was saying, Dai put his hand over hers. "You're grieving over your friend, the big man, aren't you?"

"Yes, Tramere was the best friend I ever had except for my parents. I don't know how I'll get along without him."

"You know, Sanara, I somehow knew, as soon as I saw him, that he was my brother."

"Tramere was your *brother?* Why, you're nothing alike."

"Oh, I don't mean according to blood. But those of us who are Christians feel that all other Christians are brothers—or sisters. We're all part of the family of God. So no matter how different someone is in appearance, we know we're really of the same family."

"I think that's so sweet. I never heard of anything like that." She drew her hand away. "I—I will miss him all the same. All my life he's been there when I needed him."

Slowly Dai nodded his head. "I know what you're thinking. I've lost friends to death, too. There was a man that lived a long time ago. He wrote books for boys and girls and for adults too. His name was Lewis. Anyway, this man said once, "Christians never say good-bye." He smiled at her warmly. "And I think that's rather fine, don't you?"

"I don't really understand it. Everybody says good-bye at some time. "

"It simply means that we Christians believe that when we die we go to heaven."

"Heaven. Oh, is that one of the planets?"

Dai blinked with surprise. It never ceased to amaze him that people actually did not know of the Bible or of God's dealings with His people through Jesus. He said, "Come over here and sit down, Sanara.

I know you're disturbed, and things have been happening. It might help you with your feelings about your friend if you understood where he is."

Sanara, seeming mystified, followed him to a small couch covered with tan leather. She sat on it, looked across at him, and waited, apparently ready to listen very carefully.

Dai soon realized that Tramere had already told Sanara something of the Christian God and His Son, Jesus. So he outlined briefly his belief in the Bible as the record of the word of God. He spoke of Jesus and His death. He told her of the crucifixion and saw that she was moved.

"And this man Jesus. He was the Son of God," she said, her eyes fixed on his. "Tramere told me this, but I didn't understand."

"Yes, He was. His mother was a simple Jewish girl, but His Father was the Almighty God."

"But He died! How is it possible that the Son of God could die?"

"Because He became a man just like us, Sanara. And He died for our sins."

"For mine too?"

"Yes, for yours. And for every human being in the whole cosmos."

"I think that's wonderful. I didn't know anyone could love like that."

"Jesus did. And the Bible says God loved the world so much that He gave His only Son—Jesus—so that anybody who believes in Him should not perish but have everlasting life."

"Does it really say that?"

"Yes, it does, over and over again in one way or another. But I haven't told you the best part," Dai said, excitement in his voice. "After Jesus died on the cross for our sins, He was put into a tomb. He stayed there for three days. Then, on the third day, God raised Him from the dead. He's alive again!"

"Really?"

"Really. He was seen by many people."

"Then, where is He now?" Sanara asked earnestly.

"The Bible tells us that one day He gathered His friends on a hillside and spoke to them, and then He went up into heaven—without a spaceship, I might add. He just went back to be with His Father, Almighty God."

Sanara sat quietly for a while. "And if I'm a Christian, I can go to be with Him—in the place where Tramere is?"

"Yes, that's what being a Christian is. It's belonging to Jesus now, so that, when it comes time to die, you simply change locations. One moment you're here—the next moment you're in the presence of the Lord."

"I—I think I'd like that."

The next few minutes became a time that Dai would never forget. He had a New Testament in his pocket. He took it out and went over Scripture after Scripture with the princess. Finally he asked her quietly, "Would you like to become a Christian, Sanara?"

"Yes, I would."

"Then I'm going to pray for you, and as I pray I want you to pray—aloud or silently in your own heart, whichever you wish. All you need to tell God is that you know you've done wrong and ask Jesus to be your Savior. And the Bible says He will."

Dai bowed his head and prayed. He'd never prayed so earnestly in his life, for he felt a special love for this girl whom he had saved from death.

When he opened his eyes, he saw that she seemed to be silently praying. Tears were coming down her cheeks.

He waited for a moment, then asked, "Have you asked Jesus to save you?"

"Yes, and I know that He has. He said He would." And there was joy in her face that he had not seen there before. "Oh, Dai, I know that something is different."

"Praise the Lord!" Without consciously thinking about it, Dai reached out with both arms and gave her a hug. For one joyous moment they clung to one another.

It was at that moment that Raina walked in. She stood looking at the two clasped in each other's arms, and her face changed. Something came to her eyes, and her lips tightened. She turned blindly and left the room without saying a word.

Dai and Sanara never even knew I was there, she thought angrily. She walked stiffly down the corridor until she came to her cabin. She spoke to the voice lock, then stepped inside. As the door closed, she threw herself on her bunk and began to weep as if her heart would break.

14
A New Day Dawns

Dai Bando and Sanara were standing on the very top level of the High Castle, looking downward. The green countryside that spread before them was intersected by blue streams that crisscrossed the now verdant plain. Far off, a large lake received the light of the sun and cast a bright, azure glow over that part of the world.

"It's a beautiful planet, Sanara," Dai said, leaning on the massive stones that formed the top of the wall.

Captain Edge and the *Daystar* crew had spent a pleasant week at the High Castle, and the days had gone by quickly. Most of the time Dai was in the company of Sanara and Bronwen Llewellen. The three of them were studying the Bible, and Sanara had soaked up knowledge of the Lord like a sponge. He looked over at her fondly, suddenly wanting to run his hand over her golden hair.

It was good he did not, for at that moment Commandant Lee joined them on the lookout. Today she was wearing a flowing purple gown with white accents on the collar and sleeves, rather than her usual uniform. There were no insignias on this gown. She liked to wear civilian clothes as often as possible. Lee was a woman of dignity, but a smile was on her face.

"Are you two enjoying the view?"

"Yes, we are, Commandant," Dai said. "It's beautiful, isn't it?"

Gazing out over the beautiful scenery, Winona Lee

said, "I don't know of anything more beautiful anywhere in the cosmos. You're fortunate to live in a place like this, Princess."

"We would not be living at all if it had not been for you, Commandant Lee."

"I only wish we could have come sooner," Lee said with regret. "Many of your people died because we could not get here more quickly."

Sanara shook her head, and her golden hair cascaded around her shoulders. "We must not think like that. I've learned from Dai and from his aunt that the God of the Bible is in charge of all things. I even memorized one of the Scriptures from the Bible that says all things are working together for the good of those who love God."

Commandant Lee blinked with surprise. "You have become an expert in the Bible in a short time!"

"No, I'm not that, but my parents and I both understand that God used the Intergalactic Fleet to save our planet. Otherwise, we would have been destroyed by those horrible creatures."

While the two women talked, Dai stood slightly back, listening. He was conscious of how attached he had gotten to Sanara in a brief time. As she talked with the Commandant, he was thinking, *I've never felt this close to a girl before. I wonder why I feel like this.* He thought it must have something to do with that dream he had experienced.

And then Commandant Lee turned to him. "I must congratulate you, Dai, on your courage. Sanara has told me how you were personally responsible for saving her life."

Dai ducked his head. "I think God was in it," he said.

"You should have seen him, Commandant," Sanara

said with excitement in her blue eyes. "He acted like those Lo'custra were nothing but bugs. You never saw such strength and courage."

"I know. I wish we had a thousand just like this young man."

Sanara smiled at Dai. "I don't think," she said warmly, "that there *are* any more like this one. Not even one more!"

At the close of the week, representatives from every tribal nation on Capella gathered at the High Castle. Brutarius, Anmoir, Sanara, and Commandant Lee were sitting together in the Great Tramere Hall. The assembly hall had been renamed in honor of the big man who had lost his life protecting the princess. Dai Bando had been invited to sit with them.

"He will never be forgotten," Sanara said quietly to Dai. "Not just by naming the great hall after him, either. It will be written in the history of our peoples that he gave his life for his princess." She turned to look at him and said gravely, "And I will see him again someday, thanks to you for leading me to Christ."

Dai smiled. He wanted to take her hand, but the leaders of the tribal nations were now presenting themselves before the royal family.

Everyone waited breathlessly when Lord Miterlan, who had led the civil war, arose.

Miterlan was darker than his brother and had a more warlike bearing. He wore a uniform of dark green with a single gold emblem on his breast. At his side was a magnificent sword, the hilt crested with jewels of red and green and blue. Now he walked forward to bow before the royal couple, as others had done.

No one knew what to expect.

Temple Cole leaned over to whisper to Captain Edge, "Is it possible that Brutarius will take his revenge now that he has his brother in his power?"

"I don't think so."

"I hope not. Miterlan has a noble bearing even though he *was* a rebel."

Miterlan paused before Suzerain Brutarius, then unexpectedly drew his sword. The bodyguards at both sides leaped to attention, quickly drawing their own weapons, but Brutarius held up his hand and waited.

Reversing the blade, Miterlan stepped forward, knelt before his brother, and held out his sword. "My lord, I yield you my sword and my life. I confess in the presence of all present that I was in error and wrong in leading my people against your authority. I ask no favors but am ready to receive whatever justice you choose to deal out."

For a few breathless moments, silence reigned over the great hall. Now everyone was waiting to see what Brutarius would do.

Suddenly, the suzerain leaped from his chair and pulled Miterlan to his feet.

"My dear brother, we have had our differences. And if you have been wrong this once, *I* have been wrong many times. But here is what I say"—he held up one hand and put the other on Miterlan's shoulder—"when the skies were falling and Capella was about to die from the invasion of the hated Lo'custra, you remained loyal to your people and to your kingdom—and to your king. Come, my brother, take your seat at the table with the rest of the lords of Capella."

Before Miterlan could move, however, Sanara suddenly stood. Every eye turned toward her, and silence fell again as she began to speak. It was the first time that the suzerain's daughter had ever spoken in public, but all knew that the future ruler of Capella was speaking.

"My people, I proclaim a day of rejoicing for the return of my uncle and all of his people to our loving care!"

A loud cheer went up, and every man raised his sword and waved it wildly in the air.

"Well, I guess the future ruler of Capella knows how to handle things," Ringo said to Heck, who was seated next to him.

"She's not a bad-looking chick, you know. Maybe I better give her a break. One of these days she's going to need a man. She's nothing but a woman, and a kingdom needs a king. How does that sound? King Hector."

"It sounds awful!" Mei-Lani said, who was sitting on the other side. "You wouldn't make any kind of a king for long. You'd eat yourself to death."

"Aw, come on, doll. Cut me some slack, will you?" Heck complained. But he could say no more, for Sanara was continuing to speak.

"We live in a new day. A new time is dawning. You all know the loyalty of the one for whom this hall has been named. The one who saved my life—Tramere. He was a man who followed the God of the Bible. I did not fully understand who that God was, but our friend Dai Bando introduced me to Him. The God of Tramere is Jesus Christ. He is my God, too, and I hope in the days to come to speak to you often about the love of God and how He has given His own Son to die for us."

As Sanara went on speaking, a strange feeling crept over Dai Bando. He well knew that he felt attachment to this girl, but he also clearly saw that her destiny lay with her own people. Somehow he knew that their ways would part.

She will remember me as the one who introduced her to Jesus, but nothing more than that. She is tied to this place, and I am tied to the Rangers. And our paths must diverge.

The thought brought sadness to Dai's heart, for he recognized that he was in effect saying good-bye to Sanara, princess of Capella.

The *Daystar* was poised for liftoff. In fact, Dai Bando was the only crew member not yet aboard. The time had come when Dai and Sanara had to say good-bye verbally, and he was still outside, standing with Sanara.

Suddenly Contessa came down from the space-ship as if sent as a messenger. She pawed at him, and he looked down at her, saying, "Go back, Contessa. I'll be there in a minute."

Sanara held out her hand, and Dai did something he had never done in his entire life. But it felt right, a courtly thing to do. Bowing over the hand, he kissed it.

"It is difficult for me to say good-bye, Dai Bando," Sanara said.

"If you ever need me, Princess, you know I will come."

"I believe you would." Tears were in her eyes as she said, "I will have many to guard me now, but you will always be my number one bodyguard."

Dai did not know what to do next. She was a princess, and he was a commoner.

But suddenly she stepped forward, held up her arms, and they hugged each other. Her lips were close to his ear, and she whispered, "I will never forget you,

Dai Bando, never! I will always care for you, my friend. Never forget that."

When she released her grip and he stepped back, a thought came to Dai briefly—*Maybe I can stay on Capella, after all.* But he knew that was wrong. He bowed again and started to leave. But when he had gone a few steps, he said loudly, "The only real body-guard any of us has is Jesus Christ."

Sanara laughed happily and waved. "I'll never for-get you, Dai."

And as Dai Bando walked aboard the *Daystar*, he thought with a sudden, piercing ache, *And I'll never forget you, Sanara.*

15
A Different Destiny

Raina was sitting at her post when Dai Bando walked into the communications center.

"Are you busy, Raina?" he asked.

"Well . . . no."

Dai pulled up a chair and sat down beside her. He fidgeted for a moment. He knew from the shortness of her reply that she was still upset with him. He had been thinking about Raina a great deal on the return journey through space. He had finally made up his mind to have a talk with her.

"I came to say something to you, Raina. I don't know how to make good speeches, but I want you to know that I like you a lot. I always have. And I would hate for anything to break up our friendship."

Raina turned her face away from him. He saw that her hands were trembling. She merely mumbled, "I'd hate it, too."

Dai waited, hoping that she would say more. When he saw that she was not going to, he reached over and touched her arm.

She didn't move.

He said, "Could you look at me, please, Raina?" He waited until she had turned in his direction, and then he saw the hurt in her eyes.

"First, I think I ought to tell you that I haven't had all that many friends, so I can't afford to lose any." He chewed his lip before going on. "I think Sanara would have been a good friend. But looking back at it now, I see that God just put me in her way to help her find Jesus. I know you saw me hugging her—I could see your reflection in the port—and you thought it was more personal, but it was just a friendly hug. That was all."

"Is that all it was, Dai? It looked to me as if it meant a lot more than that."

"I was hugging Sanara because she had just given her heart to the Lord! It was . . . well . . . it was the same as I would have done with a guy, I guess. I just put my arms around her because I was happy for her. But I could tell you were hurt. And I'm sorry."

"I guess I was hurt a little bit. Foolish, wasn't it? You've got a right to hug anybody you want to."

"Do I really?"

"Of course, you do."

As always, Dai's moves were so quick that no one could parry them. Suddenly his arm was around Raina. She struggled for a moment, then looked up and saw that he was smiling at her.

"Well," he said, "you said I had the right to hug anybody, so I'm just taking advantage of my rights."

"Oh, Dai," she said in a disgusted tone. "Let me go!"

He released her, then said, "You know, Raina, I've told you that I needed to have good Christian friends and that you were the finest one I know. Maybe you wanted more than that. I don't know. But I'll say it again. I've never met a girl like you in my whole life."

Raina sat very still. "Really, Dai?" she said softly.

"Really and truly."

He thought a while and then added, "As I said before, I think Sanara and I would have been real good friends, but she's got a different destiny. She'll spend the rest of her life there on Capella, doing a good job ruling her people. And I feel that's not what God wants for me. I really don't know yet *what* He wants," he said, "but I was hoping you'd help me find it."

"I hope . . . well, I want to help if I can, Dai, but—"

"Hey, what's going on in here—a little high-powered smooching?"

Dai jumped up as if he had been burned, and both he and Raina whirled toward the door of the communications area.

Mr. Hector Jordan strolled in. He had a half-eaten banana in one hand. The missing half was obviously stuffed into one cheek. In the other hand was an enormous cookie. He took a huge bite out of the cookie and said around the bite, "You're wasting your time with this guy, doll. I've told you that before."

"Heck, please . . . could you . . . we were having a private conversation!" Raina cried.

"Well, to tell the truth—"

But at that moment, the half cookie in Heck's left hand disappeared.

"Hey—what's going on?"

Heck wheeled around to see Contessa gulping down his cookie in one bite. She was also furiously wagging her tail. As soon as she had swallowed the last morsel, she planted her big paws on Heck's shoulders and shoved him back against the bulkhead.

"Get this beast off of me!" Heck howled. He held his banana at arm's length and with the other hand tried to push the dog away. "She's fallen for me like all females do! Get her off of me!"

But Dai and Raina were both laughing at Heck's predicament.

Big as Heck was, Contessa still outweighed him. Beside that, she was tremendously strong. She held him tightly pinioned against the bulkhead while she licked his face.

Finally Heck was able to fish a candy bar out of his pocket. He said, “Here! Take this, you beast, and leave me alone!”

At that point, Dai suddenly seized Raina’s hand. “Come on. These two want to be alone,” he said. He stepped quickly out of Communications, towing Raina after him. “How about us going down to the rec room for a game of chess?”

“Sounds good to me, Dai, if that’s what you want.”

The mighty Mark V Star Drive engines relentlessly propelled the *Daystar* through the vastness of starry space. But Dai Bando and Raina St. Clair had no consciousness of the cruiser’s great speed. Side by side, they walked down the deck toward the recreation room. And they looked like any other two young people, except that they were in *Daystar* Space Ranger uniform, traveling at the speed of light.

Moody Press, a ministry of the Moody Bible Institute,
is designed for education, evangelization, and edification.
If we may assist you in knowing more about Christ
and the Christian life, please write us without obligation:
Moody Press, c/o MLM, Chicago, Illinois 60610.